MRS. MALORY
• AND THE •
ONLY GOOD LAWYER

Hazel Holt

A SIGNET BOOK

SIGNET
Published by the Penguin Group
Penguin Putnam Inc., 375 Hudson Street,
New York, New York 10014, U.S.A.
Penguin Books Ltd, 27 Wrights Lane, London W8 5TZ, England
Penguin Books Australia Ltd, Ringwood, Victoria, Australia
Penguin Books Canada Ltd, 10 Alcorn Avenue,
Toronto, Ontario, Canada M4V 3B2
Penguin Books (N.Z.) Ltd, 182–190 Wairau Road,
Auckland 10, New Zealand

Penguin Books Ltd, Registered Offices:
Harmondsworth, Middlesex, England

Published by Signet, an imprint of Dutton NAL,
a member of Penguin Putnam Inc.
Previously published in a Dutton edition.
Originally published in Great Britain as *The Only Good Lawyer* by
Macmillan General Books.

First Signet Printing, December, 1998
10 9 8 7 6 5 4 3 2 1

For Geoffrey

. . . on my knees . . .

The first thing we do,
let's kill all the lawyers.

—*King Henry VI, Part II*

•|•

He telephoned right in the middle of my favorite soap opera, something that always irritates me. Mind you, I think it's extremely unlikely that my friend Graham even knows that such programs exist, or, if he does, he'd never imagine that anyone he knew would actually be watching them.

"I've recorded it," Michael said when I eventually got back into the sitting room, "and I've put your supper in the oven."

Although he has certain faults (an airy disregard for punctuality and a strong disinclination to tidy his room), Michael is a very good son.

When I had sat down again with the congealed remains of supper on a tray on my lap, I said, "Guess who that was?"

"From your lugubrious tone it must have been someone . . . Oh God! No, not Graham!"

When I say "my friend Graham," that's not strictly accurate. He was a friend of my late hus-

band—no, well, not a *friend* exactly, just someone
he'd known ever since they were both at the College
of Law. Graham simply *attached* himself to Peter in
their first term, and although it was obvious that he
was a terrible bore, he was the sort of pathetic bore
that it is difficult to bring oneself to get rid of. Certainly my kindhearted husband couldn't. And over
a period of thirty years or so, Graham Percy has become part of our lives, and every year he has paid
us a visit. A more sensitive or perceptive person
might perhaps have noted a certain lack of enthusiasm, a rather forced joviality on our part, but Graham, like all self-centered people, sees what he
wants to see and, I'm sure, always describes us to
other people as his oldest and dearest friends and
looks forward to his visit to Taviscombe as one of
the high spots of his year.

"When we didn't hear from him at the usual time
I thought we might have got away with it this year,"
I said. "But apparently he's had some sort of virus
that laid him low for a few weeks and now . . ."

"And now he wants to visit. Oh, Ma, really, do we
have to?"

"Oh, darling, I know he's *dire*, but we can't suddenly drop him after all these years. Your father
wouldn't have."

"No, well, I suppose you're right. When's he coming? So that I can be called away suddenly on important business."

"On the twenty-first, and you know you can't

chicken out—I'm afraid you're one of the reasons he likes coming."

"Oh, God! All those endless reminiscences—'My Nine Hundred and Ninety-Nine Most Interesting Cases'! I wouldn't mind, but he's a lousy solicitor—Pa always said so. And I can't stand his 'When you've been in the law as long as I have, my boy'!"

Michael is now an assistant solicitor in his father's old firm and, therefore, particularly vulnerable to Graham's inexhaustible and inexorable loquacity.

"Well," I said soothingly, "it's only for four days. Let me see. The first night, just us; the second night I'll ask Rosemary and Jack (though I do feel a bit mean about inflicting him on them), and the third night, Anthea and Ronnie. The last night he'll want to take us out to dinner."

Michael groaned. "That'll be the Esplanade again!"

The Esplanade is Taviscombe's largest hotel, characterized by a kind of gloomy grandeur and not, I'm afraid, noted for the excellence of its cuisine.

"Everyone there is always over ninety," Michael said. "Talk about the living dead! If we've got to go out, do, for heaven's sake, Ma, try and point him in the direction of the Anchor or somewhere a bit more lively."

"He thinks he's giving us a treat," I said sadly. "Anyway, you only have to cope with him in the evenings; I have him all day. Oh, well, I suppose it'll have to be the usual round of stately homes—I think

Ribston Manor is open now, that'll be a new one. It's quite big, I believe, so with lunch it might take up a whole day."

"Is he coming straight from London?" Michael asked. "As if I care!"

"No, he's going to the Shelleys and the Heywoods first."

Graham's visit to us was part of the sort of royal progress he made round the country, a progress like that of a Tudor monarch, inspiring panic and dismay in equal proportions. Bryan Shelley is Deighton Professor of Classics at Oxford, and Paul and Alice Heywood (he's a distinguished author and she designs gardens) live about thirty miles away in the north of the county and are, thus, suitable stopping-off points.

"And after us he's going on to Bath to stay with Alec Patmore."

Sir Alexander Patmore, the theatrical knight, had been at school with Graham, as had Paul Heywood and Bryan Shelley, and this, together with the fact that he is their solicitor, presumably accounts for the fact that he is able to inflict these visitations on them as he does on us. We knew about Graham's visits to the Shelleys, the Heywoods, and to Alec Patmore since he is always anxious to give his new hosts a description of the minutiae of the preceding visit.

"Oh, Lord! We'll have to hear all about Paul's new book and Alice's bees, not to mention how degenerate the youth of Oxford is these days."

"Oh, well," I said philosophically, "it's only for a

few days once a year. Can you wind back the video and I'll see what I missed."

I rang up my friend Rosemary next morning and tentatively mentioned Graham's visit.

"Rescue operation?" she asked.

"Yes, please. I hate to ask, but it *would* be a life-saver."

"Oh, all right. What are friends for? Jack can talk to him about tax law and give you a little breather."

"Jack's marvelous with bores," I said admiringly. "He simply tanks right over them!"

Jack, as well as being my friend Rosemary's husband, is an accountant and a local councillor, and therefore (on all three counts) adept at making his views heard against any opposition.

"Graham's coming on the twenty-first, so if you *could* make it the twenty-second, that's a Thursday, that would be marvelous. Though the twenty-third would be okay."

"Hang on a second while I look . . . yes, the twenty-second's fine. We've got a wretched dinner in Taunton on the twenty-third. Some sort of chartered surveyors' bash. Do you feel like a trip to Exeter to help me buy a new frock? Some fool spilt red wine on the skirt of my faithful old blue at that do at the Grand, and I simply can't get into my little black number anymore, so I haven't a thing to wear."

"Oh, yes, that would be lovely, and then I can pop into Marks and Spencer and lay in a stock of goodies to ease the catering while Graham's here. He never seems to realize that one has to *prepare* food for a dinner party, however small, and expects me to be there listening to him banging on when I should be in the kitchen doing something interesting with balsamic vinegar. Or else he follows me out there and stands just behind me, so that whenever I turn round to get a saucepan or try to get to the sink with floury hands he's always *there*!"

"Oh, I know! Jack's sister Evelyn is just the same—worse, really, because she's always saying, 'Now do tell me what I can do to help' until I want to scream."

I enjoyed my shopping trip with Rosemary, but I must confess that my enjoyment was overshadowed by the prospect of Graham's visit, which hung over my consciousness like a gloomy cloud. As I resentfully vacuumed the spare room with extra care to get up the dog hairs from the rugs (Tris and Tess like to retreat there whenever Foss, my Siamese, proves too troublesome) and picked off, one by one, the cat hairs that had mysteriously appeared on the embroidered runner on the chest of drawers (Foss in an investigative mood), I thought of all the things I might have been doing over the next few days (two books to review and an article on Emily Eden to write) instead of listening to Graham droning on.

———

"Well, Sheila, it's good to see you. And Michael, too. How's the law, eh?"

"Fine, thanks," Michael said politely and listened with an apparent show of interest to a long-winded description of a complicated trust that Graham had recently read about in the *Law Quarterly* (sometimes I'm really proud of the way I brought up my son).

"I'll just see how dinner's coming along," I said and thankfully escaped into the kitchen.

Drinks helped a little—a large gin and tonic for me, beer for Michael, and whisky for Graham ("Just a *little* water then, please, Sheila, if it's a single malt.")—and I began to think that it wasn't going to be so bad after all and poor old Graham was really rather a sad figure one ought to be sorry for.

He had never married, had, indeed, never had any sort of attachment so far as we knew. There was an elder sister, Dulcie, but she and her husband had both died some years ago and Graham's only relative was her son, Clive. We knew quite a lot about Clive since Graham was very proud of him and had told us at great length about his achievements in the City (highly profitable), his house at Gerrards Cross (detached, five bedrooms and a tennis court), his wife (an accountant in her own right), his son (a prodigy at five), and his au pair (Swedish).

Dinner was successful because I had remembered that Graham had a fondness for nursery puddings and had made a rather good steamed chocolate sponge. When we were sitting over our coffee ("It is decaffeinated, I hope, Sheila. I cannot sleep at all if I have caffeine in any form after three o'clock in the afternoon), I said to Michael, "Weren't there some papers you had to look over before tomorrow?"

He gave me a grateful look and disappeared to his room, from whence I could hear muted sounds that I hoped Graham wouldn't identify as a particularly violent television detective series. I needn't have worried. Having got the full attention of a one-to-one audience, Graham embarked on a recitation of all the events of his stay with the Heywoods.

"I thought Paul had aged considerably since I saw him last year. Of course, he is almost a year older than I am, but he takes no exercise."

Graham is a great walker and never tires of telling one how he always walks to his office in Holborn from his flat in Bayswater ("Across Hyde Park, rain or shine, I can do it in under the hour") and nearly every weekend he drives out to some spot in Buckinghamshire or Berkshire and walks over whatever wide open spaces are available. He is a short man, but strong and wiry, with dark hair, now streaked with gray, and a small, bristly moustache.

He looked at me reproachfully.

"It is a great pity you don't walk more, Sheila. It doesn't do to let oneself go at our age."

It was a source of annoyance to Graham that I would never go for long tramps with him over Exmoor ("All this magnificent countryside right on your doorstep and you take no advantage of it!"). But that was one thing I was not prepared to do (impossible to think of having to listen to Graham *and* struggle for breath going up Dunkery Beacon), so pleading rheumatism in my foot, I managed to avoid that particular horror. However, while he was with us, it was a tradition that Graham always went for a walk by the sea early in the morning—to get up an appetite for breakfast, as he inevitably said.

I thought it better to change the subject.

"And how was Alice?" I asked.

"Very eccentric these days," he said severely. "She is quite obsessed with those bees, and now she has taken to keeping goats as well—most unpleasant creatures."

Needless to say, Graham does not care for animals, and it was another source of irritation about his visits that the dogs had to be kept in the kitchen and Foss (whom it is impossible to control) had to be persuaded that he preferred to live in my bedroom, having all his meals and an earth tray up there. I had to leave the window open so that he could come and go over the adjacent garage roof, an exercise he invariably indulged in around four in the morning when he would land on my bed with a terrific thump, waking me from a fitful sleep. This modus vivendi worked to a limited extent, but occasional Siamese bellows indicated that he was not entirely satisfied with the arrangement.

"I suppose Alice is into self-sufficiency," I said. "Very admirable, really."

"Quite unnecessary." Graham had this habit of abrupt contradiction that effectively snipped off the thread of a conversation before it could really get started.

"So what about Paul's new book?" I tried again. "His last one, that life of Garrick, was absolutely brilliant!"

"A succès d'estime only, I fear. I cannot believe that he made very much money out of it. And the amount of time required to write a book of that nature—it's not at all an economic proposition."

"I always thought that Garrick book ought to have won the Whitbread, it was so much better than that thing by Millicent Robertson."

"I believe all these so-called literary prizes are *arranged* in some way. I imagine it depends, like most things, on whom you know."

"Oh, no!" I protested. "I'm sure that's not true!"

Graham smiled pityingly, as if to a small child who has made a ridiculous remark, but made no other comment.

I tried again.

"How were Bryan and Odette?"

"I only saw Bryan," he said disapprovingly. "Odette was away again in France."

Odette is French and occasionally visits her family. I admired the way she had contrived to arrange her trip to Antibes to coincide with Graham's visit, though I don't imagine Bryan was too pleased.

"I really cannot see how a marriage can work," Graham continued, "if one of the partners is always away."

"I don't think she goes away that often," I protested. Graham ignored my interruption.

"Bryan was very disorganized and his domestic arrangements left a great deal to be desired. In fact, if I hadn't already informed Paul and Alice of the proposed date of my arrival, I would have been very tempted to cut short my visit. There was some sort of woman who came in to clean, but that was all. Bryan was in College all day," he continued, his voice sharpening with displeasure, "so I was obliged to make my own arrangements for food and so forth. Of course I dined with him in Hall in the evenings."

"That was nice," I said.

"The food, indeed, was excellent, but I found the young Fellows at St. Barnabas most tiresome—very opinionated and quite unwilling to listen to anything their elders had to say."

"Oh, dear."

"And," Graham continued his litany of complaint, "I was obliged to get my own breakfast! 'Just forage for yourself,' Bryan said! As you know, I am an early riser and I do like to go for a good walk before breakfast. I therefore left the house at seven o'clock and walked in Port Meadow—their house, you will remember, is at Wolvercote—but when I returned at eight o'clock, Bryan had already left for College. Every morning! Most uncivil."

I suppressed a smile at the thought of Bryan (not, I recalled, normally an early riser) scrambling to get out of the house before his guest got back.

"Now I am in Taviscombe," Graham said graciously, "I shall look forward to my usual walk by the sea."

"I've put an electric kettle and things to make an early morning cup of tea by your bed. And of course," I said dutifully, "I'll have breakfast ready by the time you come back."

When Graham made his report on his stay in Taviscombe—as he inevitably would, to whatever reluctant audience he could command—I wouldn't want it thought that *I* had been in any way lacking, on the domestic front, at any rate.

· 2 ·

Ribston Manor is a mixture of styles and periods, being originally a modest Tudor manor house whose subsequent owners built on bits here and there as the fancy took them. Thus, in addition to the original building—soft rosy brick and bleached silver-gray beams—there is a fine seventeenth-century facade (with Dutch influence), an elegant Georgian wing, and a vast Gothic library and chapel stuck on at the side as a Victorian afterthought. However, the house stands in large and very beautiful grounds whose benign influence somehow blends the disparate parts into a surprisingly harmonious whole.

"Shall we go round the garden first?" I asked Graham. "While the weather's nice. It looks as if it might rain later."

The fact that Graham lives in a second-floor flat, with not even a window box, doesn't prevent him from having very definite views about horticulture, which he propounds with the air of an expert.

"Those trees and shrubs should be cut right back," he said briskly. "Let a little light in."

Since we were at that moment walking along a superbly laid-out avenue of beeches, with interlacing branches meeting overhead in perfect symmetry, and whose verges were planted with fine azaleas and rhododendrons, I didn't feel able to reply.

We emerged into the garden proper and wandered along the terrace to the water garden where the early irises were just coming into bloom.

"Very dangerous, all this open water," Graham said. "If a child were to fall in and drown, they could be liable for quite a considerable sum in compensation."

"Aren't those irises magnificent?" I said, hoping to avert a lecture on liability in the law. "I think those bronze and yellow ones are my favorites."

He reluctantly followed my pointing finger. "Very nice," he said perfunctorily. "It must cost a fortune to keep these gardens stocked. I suppose the family must have considerable private means—the money they make from letting in the public wouldn't nearly cover the upkeep of a place like this. Though, I must say, I thought the entrance fee of four pounds fifty was excessive."

"Well," I said placatingly, since Graham had insisted on buying the tickets, "it was for the house *and* gardens. Shall we go in now?"

Once inside, I was able to edge Graham into conversation with one of the guides and have a little wander on my own. This was just as well, since I knew from past experience that Graham and I approach the business of looking around in totally opposite ways. In museums and stately homes my friend Rosemary and I favor what we call the darting-about method—in other words, wandering about in a disorganized way looking at things that catch our fancy. We also never read the guidebook as we go, preferring to absorb the *spirit* of the place and reading about it after. This often means that we find we've missed quite important things ("Did *you* see the seventeenth-century strap-work? Perhaps that was it in the funny little room upstairs with the picture of that child with the sweet dog"), but I think, on the whole, we enjoy ourselves and get more out of things than those conscientious people who plod round with their noses stuck in the guidebook, hardly raising their heads to see the beauties listed there. Graham was definitely a plodder.

He caught up with me in the hall as I was examining the intricately carved Jacobean staircase.

"Most interesting," he said. "Did you know that they reckon to make enough from the sale of plants to pay the wages of at least one of the full-time gardeners?"

"Fancy," I said. "Do look at this beautiful carving—there's a deer, do you see, just there, and a couple of hounds and masses of twiggy branches and things. Isn't it gorgeous!"

Graham turned the pages of his guidebook, the better to appreciate the object in question, and I took the opportunity to slip into the old kitchen and meditate on the problems involved in cooking with such primitive apparatus. Though, I must say, one of my father's old friends had an Elizabethan farmhouse where we used to go and stay when I was a child, and his housekeeper always used to roast the Sunday joint on a clockwork spit in front of the fire. I can still remember the heavenly smell as the outside of the meat crisped up, and hear the spitting of the fat as it splashed from the tin placed underneath into the flames. The thought of this made me feel hungry, so I went in search of Graham to suggest we might have an early lunch.

"They've turned the old stables into a sort of restaurant, so if we go now it should be nice and empty. Then we can do the rest of the house afterwards."

The dish of the day was chicken curry, and since there was no possibility of Graham's eating *that* ("Curry in a proper Indian restaurant is one thing, Sheila, but in a place like this I really do not think I would care to trust it"), we both had a ham salad, which was very nice with home-cooked ham and proper mayonnaise.

"So how is Alec Patmore?" I asked. "I did read in one of the papers that he wasn't at all well. Certainly I haven't seen him in anything for ages."

"Very sad," Graham said, breaking a bread roll with precision. "I believe it's a form of arthritis. Progressive. He's in a wheelchair now."

"Oh, how awful! He was such a brilliant actor. I think his Iago was the best I ever saw, and that last film he did—you know, the one set in India—was magnificent."

"Fortunately," Graham said, "he did make quite a considerable sum of money from the last few films he made, which is just as well, since I imagine he will have to go into a nursing home before long, and you know how expensive *they* are."

"Who looks after him now?"

"He has a manservant, the person who used to be his 'dresser.'" Graham put the unaccustomed word between quotation marks. "Quite efficient, I believe. Certainly when I stayed there last he seemed to have things well organized, and when I proposed myself for this visit, there seemed to be no problem."

"What's he like, Alec Patmore? As a person, I mean."

Graham seemed somewhat at a loss.

"As a person?" he echoed. "Well, much as anyone else, I suppose. Rather affected in some ways— but I imagine all actors are like that. Having known him for so long, it is difficult to pin him down, as it were."

"Of course, you were at school together, weren't you? And Paul Heywood and Bryan Shelley. I can't imagine you all as small boys."

"Well, hardly small—it was not a preparatory school, after all."

"Oh, you know what I mean. What were you all like?"

"Much as other boys."

"But were you all especial friends? I suppose you must have been, since you've kept in touch all this time. And, of course, you were all up at Oxford together."

"Such things do create a bond," Graham said sententiously. "Certain things one has in common. A band of brothers."

I have always imagined that it was the others who formed the band and Graham tagged on, immovable as a burr, in his usual fashion.

"Of course, Alec and I do have certain family connections. His mother was a Percy on *her* mother's side, so we share a common forebear, though her side of the family was one of the remoter cadet branches with a more distant descent from the true Northumberland line than my own."

Graham is a genealogy bore and, being also something of a snob, forever going on about his relationship (very remote it seems to me) with the Dukes of Northumberland.

"How interesting," I said mendaciously. "What does that make you? Third cousins, thrice removed or something?"

He gave a bleak smile at what he perceived to be a joke. "I have worked out the relationship, but, of course, it does involve five separate family trees. If

you are interested I will send you a copy of the document. I had several made when I wrote an article
about the Percy line for the *Journal of Northern Ge-
nealogical Studies*."

"I didn't know you'd rushed into print, Graham."

"The article has not yet appeared," he replied,
"since they had too much material for that year.
However, the editor, who is an acquaintance of
mine—we belong to the same club—assured me
that it will undoubtedly be published sometime in
the future. Now, if you do not want any coffee, let
us go and look at the library. Apparently the exte-
rior was greatly influenced by Pugin."

The next two days were filled with similar expe-
ditions to other houses, which was the only way I
could think of entertaining him in the spell of rainy
weather that followed, and in the evenings my
faithful friends rallied round.

"Only one more day to go," Michael said when
we were loading the dishwasher. Graham had gone
up to bed immediately after Anthea and Ronnie
had gone ("I will turn in now, Sheila. I want to be
up especially early tomorrow, since I want to have
a really *good* walk before breakfast now that the
weather has improved").

"Thank goodness," I said. "I really am quite exhausted from all that *listening*—well, not even listening really, just letting it all wash over me, but
equally tiring. And thank you, darling, for being so

good and patient. You were splendid tonight, letting him tell you about that tedious case with, what was it? Wandsworth Borough Council?"

"Well, all you need to do is say, 'Yes, I see,' at intervals. Anyway, Ronnie was splendid, banging on about that new bypass thing—that took up quite a bit of the evening."

"And," I added, "Anthea riding her hobbyhorse about the Common Market—they were certainly on the same wavelength about *that*!"

Michael yawned deeply. "Well," he said, "I'm off to bed. You'd better have an early night, too, if you've got to get up early to make this enormous breakfast he'll be expecting."

"Yes, I will—I'll just see to the animals. I do so *pray* tomorrow will be fine. He was really upset that he couldn't get his early-morning walks yesterday and today."

It was a lovely morning and I breathed a sigh of relief as I drew back the curtains to see the clear blue skies and the fresh washed beauty of the countryside on a perfect late spring day.

When I got down I saw that Graham had already gone out. His car was gone—he always drove himself down to the seafront and began his walk from there. I hummed cheerfully to myself as I cut the rind off the bacon, trimmed the bread for toast, put out the eggs ready for poaching ("Not fried, please, Sheila, or scrambled, just lightly poached—so much more digestible"), and measured the coffee into the machine. Happily I took up Foss's plate of chopped rabbit and put it on the windowsill, his preferred eating place in my room.

"There you are, Foss. Last day. Back to normal tomorrow."

Foss gave a loud wail, possibly of agreement or, more likely, satisfaction at the appearance of his food. Then I went downstairs to feed the dogs and turn them out of doors into the bright morning sunshine, where they ran about barking madly with excitement at being outside again after several days shut up in the house because of the rain.

Michael came down at about eight o'clock and I cooked his breakfast and had a piece of toast myself.

"I'll have my second piece of toast and my coffee with Graham when he comes in," I said. "It's more sociable."

Michael left at a quarter to nine.

"He's certainly having a good long walk," he said. "Do you think he's all right?"

"Oh, yes," I said, glad to have the kitchen to myself for a bit longer to clear up Michael's breakfast things. "I expect he's gone right along to Dunster Beach—it's quite a way. I expect he's making the most of being by the sea. He always says the sea air is good for his sinuses."

By nine-thirty I was beginning to get worried and kept going to the window whenever I heard a car. I made myself some toast and poured a cup of coffee, thinking, in the superstitious way that one does, that it might make him come. But it didn't. I put my cup and saucer and plate into the dishwasher and went back to the window again. It was nearly ten o'clock now and I was very uneasy indeed. I felt I should go and look for Graham, but he didn't have a key and if—when—he did turn up, he wouldn't be able to get in.

On a sudden resolve I tore a piece of paper from the telephone pad and scribbled on it:

Gone to look for you. Wait in the summerhouse.
S.

I cellotaped it to the front door. If it was an open invitation to burglars that was just too bad.

I shut the dogs in the house, snatched up a jacket, and got my car out. I drove slowly down to the seafront, expecting to see round every corner Graham's familiar dark blue Rover. But there was no sign of him.

The Promenade was quite busy. Although it wasn't the beginning of the season yet, there were some early holidaymakers, mostly elderly, ambling happily about in the welcome sunshine, and a few bikers in black leathers astride their formidable-looking machines. Taviscombe, for some reason, is a favorite place for bikers, and when they first appeared a few years ago, there was some disquiet in the town and murmurings among the older residents about Mods and Rockers. But they were peaceful enough, seeming content to drive slowly back and forth along the seafront, pausing occasionally to sit back on their massive saddles and eat their sandwiches and drink their cans of Coca-Cola, so that now everyone took them for granted as part of the summer scene.

I was driving toward the harbor but was stopped by a young policeman, who waved me down.

"Sorry, madam, we've had to block off the road from here." He indicated the white tape barrier that had been stretched across the road.

"Why?" I asked. "What's the matter?"

"There's been an incident," he said importantly.

"Incident?" I began to feel a sense of panic. "What sort of incident?"

"I'm afraid I can't say."

"Please," I said urgently, "I'm trying to find someone—he went for a walk ages ago and hasn't come back. I'm afraid something might have happened to him."

The young man leaned in at the open window.

"A gentleman? What age of person would that be, then?"

"About my age—a bit older."

"I see, madam. If you'd kindly stay here for a moment . . ."

I turned off my engine and watched as he walked away toward a group of men at the far end of the quay. I strained my eyes to see if one of the cars parked down there was Graham's, but it was too far away for me to see properly. There was a fair amount of activity going on—a couple of police cars and an ambulance and people moving in and out of a sort of shelter made of plastic sheets. I had a kind of sick fear—it looked as if Graham had had an accident, perhaps he'd been knocked down by a car—we all said that they went far too fast round that final bend before the roundabout at the end of the quay. I was getting really agitated now and had just got out of the car to see for myself what was happening when I saw that a man was coming toward me. It was Roger Eliot, my friend Rosemary's son-in-law, our local chief inspector.

"Sheila! What on earth are you doing here?"

"Oh, Roger, what's happened—is it an accident?" I said incoherently.

He took me gently by the arm and led me back toward my car.

"Now then, what is it? Tell me all about it."

I took a deep breath and tried to pull myself together and gather my thoughts.

"I've got a friend staying with me," I said, speaking slowly and carefully, "and he went out for a walk very early this morning and he hasn't come back. I'm worried in case something might have happened to him."

"What is his name?"

"Graham—Graham Percy."

Roger looked grave and was silent for a moment. Then he said slowly, "I don't know how to put this— I'm sorry, Sheila, but I'm afraid he's dead."

"Dead?" Although I had half expected to hear that something dreadful had happened, I was still unprepared for the blunt statement. "What happened? Was it an accident?"

Roger shook his head. "No. It wasn't an accident. It seems that he was murdered."

· 3 ·

For a few moments I stared at Roger, unable to take in what he had said. "But that's impossible. Who on earth would want to murder Graham? There must be some mistake—where did you find him? How did you know his name?"

"A couple walking their dog discovered him in one of the shelters on the Promenade here. We found a letter addressed to a Graham Percy in his pocket."

"How did he .. ?" I couldn't complete the sentence.

"He died from a stab wound to the chest."

"But *why*?"

"Sheila," Roger asked, "would he have had his wallet on him?"

"I don't know for certain, but, yes, I'm sure he would."

"That's probably it, then. He didn't have one when we found him."

"You mean it was just a robbery—he was killed for a few pounds and a couple of credit cards? Oh, God, how awful!"

Roger opened the door of the car and pushed me gently into the seat. "Just sit quietly for a bit," he said. "Are you all right? Would you like me to get someone to drive you home? I'd do it myself, but—well—I'm a bit tied up here."

I shook my head. "No, no. I'll be all right in a minute."

"Look, you go home now and I'll come out and see you later. There is just one thing, though. We'll need someone to identify him. Shall I call Michael?"

"No," I said quickly, "don't do that. I'll do it." I braced myself. "Do you want me to do it now?"

Roger shook his head. "No. The scene of crime people haven't finished yet, and anyway, it would be better if you did it later—you know. I'll arrange all that when I see you."

Presumably Roger thought I might find it less harrowing in more clinical surroundings, and I was grateful for his consideration. "Yes, well . . ." I said uncertainly. "I'll go back now and ring Michael and tell him what's happened."

Roger looked at me searchingly. "You're sure you're okay?"

"Yes." I gave him a weak smile. "Still a bit stunned, actually. I suppose it'll sink in properly later."

"I'll be along in a couple of hours," Roger said. "Meanwhile, hot, sweet tea—or something stronger!"

I took a last look at the group of figures busy round the plastic sheeting and suddenly thought of something. "Oh, Roger. What about his car? He usually parks it that end of the Promenade when he goes for a walk. I suppose it's still there. What should we do about it?"

"We'll have to have a look at it of course, and then someone will drive it back to you. What's it like?"

He noted down the make and number that I gave him.

"Right, then, off you go."

I closed the door, turned the car round, and drove slowly back home.

My main feeling, I found, was one of guilt. Guilt that I wasn't more upset. Shocked, yes, stunned, even, but not upset. The fact that I had never really liked Graham, had found him tiresome, irritating, and boring, somehow made me feel almost worse than if I had really cared for him. I suppose it was because I wasn't grieving. And mixed in with the guilt was a kind of anger, that he should, however unwittingly, put us in this unpleasant situation.

I said as much to Michael when I telephoned him.

"I keep thinking, 'How typical of Graham!' Isn't that awful!"

"Yes, I know how you feel, but you mustn't. You'll only get worked up and make yourself ill! Now then, I'll be back for lunch, and I can take the afternoon off if you like."

"It would be marvelous if you could. Not for me,

I'm fine, really, but Roger's coming round later to give me the details, and to ask a few questions about Graham, I suppose. He may want to see you, too."

"Sure, that's okay then, I've only got old Sam Beckworth, remaking his will for the umpteenth time this afternoon, and Martin can cope with him. See you soon."

I was grateful that the need to get lunch kept me from thinking too much about what had happened. The animals, too, provided a distraction. The dogs were restless because they hadn't had their usual walk, so I let them loose in the garden, though I had to rush out and remove them from where they were investigating a somnolent hedgehog they had found (though not, I feared, before they had picked up a whole colony of fleas). And Foss, reinstated downstairs, stalked up and down the work-top, where I was trying to grate some cheese for a quick bolognese, complaining about his previous inconvenience in a muted bellow.

"Poor old Ma," Michael said sympathetically. "What a ghastly thing to happen."

"Poor old Graham," I said. "What a *wasteful* way to die!"

"I suppose you don't know the details?"

"No, just the bare fact, really. I expect Roger will fill us in when he comes."

But Roger hadn't much more to tell.

"He must have been killed sometime before eight o'clock, which is when this elderly couple"—he consulted a notebook—"a Mr. and Mrs. Quigley, found him."

"Edward and Marjorie Quigley?" I exclaimed. "I know them from the Red Cross. They've got a rather boisterous Welsh collie—I sometimes meet them dog-walking."

"I gather it was the dog who actually drew their attention to the fact that something was wrong," Roger said. "And the fact that Mr. Quigley had some first aid training was useful, too, because it meant that he knew at once that Mr. Percy was dead, so he didn't move the body at all before he called us."

"Eight o'clock," I said slowly. "Then Graham must have left the house really early. He'd gone out by the time I got down. That was about seven-thirty."

"You didn't hear the car or anything?"

"No, but then I sleep at the back of the house and he'd left his car in the drive at the front."

"How about you, Michael?"

"Sorry. I'm at the back, too."

"Anyway," I said, "Michael's what's known as a heavy sleeper!"

"Oh, well, we've still got a few statements from people who were on the Promenade. We may be able to fix times more exactly when we've been through them. And, of course, there'll be the pathology report as well."

"Did you say Graham was stabbed?" I nerved myself to ask. "Do you think he died immediately, I mean, do you think he suffered?"

"Well, as I said, I haven't seen the forensic report," Roger said, "but it seemed to me that death would have been instantaneous. We haven't found a weapon yet, but I'd say it would take quite a large knife to make a wound like that."

"A robbery that went wrong?" Michael asked.

"We must assume so." Roger turned to me. "Have you had a chance to check his room and see if his wallet is there?"

"Well, actually," I said, "I haven't been up there yet, partly, to be honest, because I couldn't face it, but partly because I thought I'd wait until you came so that things would be exactly as he left them."

"Well done. Right, then, shall we go and have a look now?"

I led the way up the stairs and opened the door of the spare room. As I saw Graham's pajamas neatly folded (he always meticulously made his bed every morning) and the shaving things laid out on the dressing table, I felt uneasy, as if Graham might come in at any moment and demand to know what we were doing with his things, and I could see that Michael felt the same. Roger, not surprisingly I suppose, obviously had no such qualms. He examined the odds and ends on the dressing table and chest of drawers, opened the wardrobe, and felt in the pockets of the suits and the coat hanging there and opened the suitcase standing beside the wardrobe, looking through some papers that were in there. After a few moments he looked up.

"No," he said, "no wallet. There's a diary, but that's just appointments, and some papers that seem to be connected with his work (I think Rosemary told me he was a solicitor), but that's all."

"Will you want to look at these things again?" I asked. "I must phone Clive, that's his nephew—I didn't think I should do it before I'd seen you because I thought I'd better have all the facts before I did. I don't know what he'll want to do about the funeral. Gerrards Cross, perhaps—that's where he lives. But he won't be able to have the body for a bit, will he—there'll have to be an inquest, I suppose. Perhaps Clive might want to come down for that. He could collect Graham's things then. Otherwise I shall have to pack them up somehow. Oh, dear . . ."

"Yes, well," Michael interrupted this meandering train of thought. "Let poor Roger get things sorted first."

"I'm sorry," I said, "I was just thinking aloud. There's so much to be *done*."

"And I'm afraid I have to ask you to do one more thing," Roger said. "Can you come down to the hospital and identify him? Though from what I can see it will only be a formality—there seems to be no doubt who he is. This afternoon, about three-thirty, if that's all right with you."

"No, look," Michael said. "There's no need for you to do that, Ma. I can do it."

"No, really," I said firmly. "It's very sweet of you,

Michael, but it's one last thing I can do for poor Graham."

We went down into the hall, where Foss emerged from the kitchen and made a beeline for Roger, determined to rub cat hairs onto the legs of his dark suit. I snatched him up, and Roger, who fortunately is an animal lover, stroked his head and said, "Delia wants a kitten. Do you think she's old enough?"

"Oh, yes, little girls are very gentle with animals. But *don't*," I added as I bundled Foss back into the kitchen and firmly shut the door, "have a Siamese. Your lives are quite complicated enough without that!"

It wasn't really as much of an ordeal as I'd expected, identifying Graham's body. It was definitely him, but the still form lying under the white sheet had that impersonality dead bodies always seem to have. The person one has known has gone and what remains is so palpably only an outer shell. Still, I said good-bye, not just to Graham but to another link with the past, another of Peter's friends gone and my own life diminished thereby.

When I got back I thought I'd better ring Clive.

"What *is* his surname?" I asked Michael. "I must have heard it a hundred times! Is it Merrison or Merivale? Merivale—I'm sure that's it, though I haven't got an address. I mean, Clive Merivale, Gerrards Cross, isn't going to be enough for Directory Enquiries, is it? I suppose I'd better go to the library, they have telephone directories for more or less everywhere there."

"Why don't you look in Graham's diary?" Michael suggested. "He's bound to have everyone's particulars neatly filed away there."

"Yes, I suppose so," I said doubtfully. "But somehow I don't really like to. A diary's such a personal thing."

Michael gave me a look of affectionate scorn. "It's okay. I'll do it." He came downstairs again with the diary in his hand. "Right, then, here's Clive's address and telephone number, and you were right, it is Merivale. Give me the telephone pad and I'll write it down for you. Oh, yes, and I suppose you'd better have Alec Patmore's as well. I mean you'd better let him know what's happened if he was expecting Graham tomorrow."

I rang Clive's number, but all I got was a disembodied voice telling me briskly to leave my message after the tone. I replaced the receiver, deciding to ring later in the evening, since there were, I felt, certain things that one couldn't put on an answerphone.

I had better luck with Alec Patmore's number. A rather cosy male voice, which I identified as Alec's former dresser, took my message and seemed disposed to talk.

"Thanks so much for letting us know. And how awful for you! Such a nasty thing to happen! Sir Alec *will* be upset. He's quite poorly now, doesn't get about much, you know. He's having his rest at the moment, but I'll tell him as soon as he wakes. I always take him a cup of tea at about four-thirty and some *very* thin slices of brown bread and butter—just like I used to do on performance days. He never takes lunch, of course, and nowadays just something quite light for supper—one of my cheese soufflés, perhaps, and a glass of white wine."

"Really?" I said, fascinated by this glimpse into the life of one of our theatrical knights.

"It's just as well," he continued, "I hadn't taken that leg of lamb out of the freezer for tomorrow—it would be too much for just the two of us . . ."

He continued in this strain for quite a while, and I realized that his was obviously a gregarious nature and he must be really rather lonely and longing for someone to chat to.

"Do you think I ought to ring the Shelleys and the Heywoods?" I asked Michael. "I mean, it might just get into the papers, and I'd hate them to see it there first."

Graham's diary provided telephone numbers for both of them. There was no reply from the Shelleys, but I got Alice Heywood and told her what had happened. She sounded surprised rather than shocked, somehow.

"What an extraordinary thing to have happened," she said. "Graham, of all people—such a *cautious* person! And in Taviscombe, too, really very odd!"

"It's all been a great shock," I said, rather put out at her reaction. "The police are still making enquiries, of course."

"The police?" she said vaguely. "Yes, I suppose they must be. Yes, well, I'll tell Paul when he comes back. He's up in London today—something to do with the book—but he should be back tonight. I expect he'll ring you then. I'm so sorry, Sheila, I have to go now. I've got a man coming to see me about the goats. Did I tell you"—her voice became quite animated—"that I'm thinking of going in for Nubians? A quite fascinating breed and so much more profitable . . ."

"Well, really," I said to Michael, "no one seems really *concerned* about poor Graham's death—all they wanted to do was tell me about cooking and goat-rearing!"

Michael gave me a wry smile. "Well," he said, "Graham's life didn't actually *impinge* on other people's, did it? Except as a source of irritation once or twice a year."

"Poor Graham!" I said. "What a dreadfully melancholy epitaph!"

"Oh, well, cheer up, Ma," Michael said, "no one could ever say that of you. Impinging is something you've got down to a fine art."

· 4 ·

Clive Merivale, when I finally got hold of him later that evening, was grave but businesslike.

"Poor Uncle Graham, what a shocking thing—it seems one isn't safe anywhere these days. Such a very distressing business for you, I am so sorry you have had to cope with all this. The inquest? I will try to come down if I can, but I have to be in Brussels for a week—I leave the day after tomorrow. But I will certainly set in motion arrangements for the funeral before I go. My mother is buried here, at All Saints, and I am sure Uncle Graham would have wished to be with her. I will, naturally, be in communication with the police, and I will send you the name and telephone number of the undertakers in case any problems should arise while I am away. Though, of course, Angela, my wife, will be here if you need to consult her. You can contact me through her if there is any emergency."

"I've telephoned the Heywoods and the Shelleys," I said. "At least Bryan Shelley wasn't in, so I'll try again later. Oh, and Alec Patmore, of course."

"Yes, yes, very good of you. I will be in touch with Uncle Graham's office tomorrow. There will be documents to be dealt with, no doubt—the will and so forth."

"I suppose everything will go to Clive," I said to Michael. "I wonder how much it will be."

"It wouldn't surprise me if Graham had quite a tidy sum stashed away," Michael replied. "I daresay Clive gave him a few tips on shares and so forth, and I know his firm does a lot of financial work. And, of course, he was a partner in a fairly high-powered outfit."

"There's the flat in Bayswater," I said. "That must be worth a bit."

"Depends on how long the lease was," Michael said thoughtfully. "But he's bound to have had quite hefty insurances as well—no, I imagine Clive will come in for something pretty substantial."

"He's Graham's only relation. I wish he could be here for the inquest, though. I've never seen him, and I've often wondered what he's like."

"Well, you'll see him at the funeral."

"Goodness, yes, I suppose I must go to that. How on earth does one get to Gerrards Cross? I wonder when it will be—I've got to go up to London to see that American editor sometime, perhaps I can combine the two. Oh, well, nothing can be arranged until after the inquest, so we'll just have to wait and see. I think I'll have another go at Bryan Shelley, he may be back by now."

I knew Bryan quite well. We were always bumping into each other at literary affairs. When I told him about Graham he seemed very upset.

"Oh, dear, I feel especially awful about it all because I wasn't very nice to him when he stayed here. I mean, Odette's away, and I'm really not very good at the domestic side of things, and Graham— well, you know how pernickety he can be!"

"I know!" I said sympathetically. "And I feel guilty, too, because I always seem to make heavy weather of his visits, resentful and rather cross!"

"I know just what you mean. . . ."

There was a brief silence while we both contemplated our own particular guilt.

"I've had a word with Clive," I said. "You know, Graham's nephew. But I don't know when the funeral will be. There's got to be an inquest, of course."

"Do you think the police will catch whoever did it?" Bryan asked.

"I don't know," I replied. "I suppose if it's some local tearaway they will, but in a seaside town like this there's always a shifting population, especially in the holiday season. Oh, dear, it's such an awful thing to have happened! And I feel sort of responsible in a way."

"Come now, Sheila! It's hardly your fault if someone gets mugged in Taviscombe, just because you happen to live there!"

"No, it's not that—though I suppose if he hadn't come to stay with us he might have been alive now. No, it's just that Graham always used to ask me to go for an early morning walk with him and I never did. I'm sure if he hadn't been alone this would never have happened."

"That's nonsense! You might as well say that if he'd overslept, if he hadn't had this passion for early rising, he'd never have gone for a walk in the first place!"

"Yes," I said, "you're right, of course. I suppose I just want to find something positive to reproach myself with."

"The fact is," Bryan said firmly, "we each found Graham tiresome in one way or another. We feel guilty (and we won't be the only ones!) because Graham is dead and we won't really miss him. The fact that he died in a particularly horrible way only accentuates the feeling. It's worse for you, you're on the spot and you've got the police to deal with."

"Well, that part of it's not too bad. The person in charge of the case is an old friend, my goddaughter's husband. He's been very kind and considerate."

"Well, let me know what's happening and about the funeral and everything. I'll try and get to that."

"I'll be glad of a little moral support. From the brief conversation I had with him on the phone, Clive doesn't sound very cosy. Will Odette be back? How long's she away for?"

"Only one more week, thank goodness, I'm sick of dining in Hall!"

Paul Heywood phoned quite late in the evening. I was faintly surprised that Alice, preoccupied with the goats, had remembered to tell him about Graham.

"Poor you," he said. "What a beastly thing to happen!"

"It is, rather."

"Fancy! Old Graham, of all people! It just goes to show!" I wasn't sure quite what it went to show, so I made no reply, and Paul went on, "Do you think the police will find who did it?"

"I hope so. They usually do in these cases, don't they?"

"Some local youth, I suppose."

"Probably."

There was a brief pause while I heard a murmur in the background.

"Alice says, what about the funeral?" he said.

"We don't know when," I replied, "because of the inquest, but it will be at Gerrards Cross, which is where his nephew lives."

"Gerrards Cross!" Paul exclaimed, as if it was somewhere in Outer Mongolia, "I don't think we can manage *that*!"

"Oh, well," I said, "I'm sure they'll understand if you can't make it. Though I don't suppose there'll be that many people there. Just us and the Shelleys—Alec Patmore's more or less housebound now, I gather. People from his firm, perhaps . . ."

"Yes, well, we'll have to see. Anyway, thanks for letting me know, Sheila. Hope to see you soon. Come over for tea one day—it's been ages since we got together."

"Touched though I am by all this sympathy," I said to Michael, "the odd word of regret for Graham wouldn't come amiss. After all, he's dead!"

"Yes, well," Michael said, "I expect they were all so grateful that it happened here and not when he was staying with them!"

Next morning, after Michael went to work, I went up into the spare room.

"I suppose I really must pack up poor Graham's things," I said to Foss, who had followed me upstairs.

I put the suitcase (of very good quality, like all Graham's things) on the bed and opened it. Inside, as Roger had found, there were a couple of files, which I put to one side. I got out the suit, cavalry twill trousers, and blazer from the wardrobe and folded them, painfully conscious that I was not performing this task with the skill and precision that Graham would have expected. I added the shirts, socks, and underwear from the drawer, shoes, slippers, pajamas, and dressing gown, hairbrush and shaving things, and so on until the case was full. Then I went to lay the files on top. As I did so, on an impulse, I took up the larger, pink file and looked at it. On the cover was a label that read "Paul Heywood: Dispute with William Campbell (Correspondence File No. 8)." I opened it and saw that the letters seemed to be about a boundary dispute, something to do with a ditch and bank that had been demolished. Presumably Graham's visit to the Heywoods had been partly business. I was surprised, though, that neither Paul nor Alice had mentioned the affair, since it looked as if it had been going on for some time—there was a reference in one of the letters to the Court of Appeal. The other file bore Bryan Shelley's name and was something to do with a Trust.

"How like Graham to combine business with pleasure," I said to Michael that evening. "I'm only surprised there wasn't a file for Alec Patmore, too—but I suppose he's too frail now to be bothered with such things."

"Did you say a boundary dispute?" Michael asked.

"Yes."

"But that's madness! What on earth was Graham thinking of to encourage Paul to embark on such a thing? They can go on forever—I've known people bankrupted by cases like that."

"Oh, dear," I said, "and it *does* seem to have been going on for a long time. It was marked File Number Eight."

"Good grief! That's terrible."

"And there were references in one of the letters I saw to the Court of Appeal."

Michael groaned. "I can't believe it! And Paul's never said anything?"

"No, nor Alice."

"I think I'd better have a look at this file."

"Oh, Michael, you can't. It's confidential. I certainly shouldn't have looked myself and you certainly can't—think of professional ethics."

"Yes, well—but, if it's been going on as long as you think, it must have cost Paul at least twenty thousand pounds by now. And if they go to appeal that'll be another twenty-five thousand, possibly more."

"No! Just for a little dispute like that!"

"Ma, going to law is an expensive business, you should know that."

"Oh, dear, how awful. But there's nothing we can do—it's not our affair."

When Roger phoned next day I assumed it was to tell us about the date of the inquest, but as soon as he began to speak I knew that it was something even more serious.

"Graham Percy's wallet was washed up on the beach this morning. Fortunately the woman who found it brought it straight to us."

"You're sure it's Graham's?"

"Oh, yes. It had all his credit cards in it." Roger paused. "Also fifty pounds in notes."

"Oh."

There was another pause and then Roger continued, "You do see, Sheila, what this means?"

"That nothing was taken."

"Yes."

"So it wasn't just a robbery that went wrong. He was murdered for some other reason."

"I'm afraid so."

I couldn't think of anything to say. The whole situation, horrible before, now seemed to take on the aspect of fantasy.

"But who would murder him here, in Taviscombe? I mean, he didn't *know* anyone here except us—" I broke off. "Roger," I said uncertainly, "you don't think *I* killed him!"

"No, Sheila, I don't think you killed him. But it does mean that I shall need you and Michael to come down to the station and make new and rather fuller statements. I won't drag Michael out of the office, but I'd be grateful if he could come in at lunchtime. And will you come now?"

"What questions did Roger ask you?" I enquired of Michael when he got home in the evening. "Do you want a beer?"

"Yes, please, I could do with something. Well, more or less what he asked you, I imagine. What was Graham's state of mind? Was he worried about anything? Who would know he would be down here? Things like that."

I poured myself an extra-large gin and tonic, also feeling the need for a little alcoholic support.

"Yes," I said, "he asked me all that. But, honestly,

I didn't notice anything different about Graham this time, did you? Just his usual, tiresome self."

"Certainly not worried or frightened," Michael agreed. "And as for people knowing about his being here, well, the field's wide open. You know how he always gives a ball-by-ball commentary on his life to anyone who'll listen!"

"That's what I told Roger," I said. "And, of course, Graham always did the same things every time he came down here—the early morning walk by the sea included. I'm sure he told the Heywoods and Paul Shelley and his nephew. Probably everyone in his office, too, I wouldn't wonder."

"That's true. One thing about bores, they're pretty easy to track down!"

"It's rather horrible to think that someone was there," I said, "just waiting their moment to . . ." I shivered. "Perhaps even watching the house."

"Not very likely," Michael said briskly. "We're pretty rural here, we'd have noticed something like that. Still, the fact remains that someone followed him down here and killed him."

"Roger seemed pretty sure it *was* someone he knew. No signs of a struggle—they were puzzled about that before, when they thought it was a robbery—so it had to be someone who could get near enough to stab him without arousing his suspicion."

"Someone he knew," I echoed. "But we come back to the question, who on earth would *want* to kill him?"

"Well, if you're looking for motive, how about Clive? He must stand to inherit a pretty hefty sum, and he does seem to have an expensive sort of lifestyle."

"He is the obvious suspect," I agreed. "And I didn't take to him at all when we spoke on the phone."

Michael smiled. "I don't think that's admissible evidence," he said.

"Well, we'll soon be able to have a proper look at him," I said. "Roger says that the inquest (day after tomorrow, by the way) will be just a formal identification and so forth, because the police will ask for an adjournment in the light of the new evidence. So they'll want Clive to come down here as soon as he gets back from Brussels. Oh, goodness, do you think we ought to offer to put him up?"

"*No*, Ma," Michael said firmly. "He can perfectly well stay at the Esplanade. He'd probably rather."

"Well," I said doubtfully, "if you're sure. It seems a bit unfriendly not even to offer." I added a little more tonic to my glass. "You don't think Roger does suspect us?" I asked. "I mean, I know he's a friend and all that, but when you come right down to it, we are the only people Graham knew here, on the spot, as it were. And neither of us has an alibi. Apart from each other, I mean."

Michael laughed. "Apart from the fact that no one, in or out of their right mind, could visualize you even treading on a beetle let alone murdering anyone, there is the little question of a motive. I mean, I know Graham was pretty irritating, but if *that* was a motive for murder, then the population of the western hemisphere would be halved overnight. And, although I found him pretty tedious, I don't think I'd go as far as murder to avoid a little boredom!"

"Yes," I said, "*we* know we haven't a motive, but Roger can't be sure of that."

"Well, there's nothing much we can do about all that," Michael said sensibly. "Try and put it out of your mind. It's up to Roger now. What's for supper? I'm starving. All this excitement certainly sharpens the appetite."

· 5 ·

I tried to take Michael's advice and concentrate on other things, but it wasn't easy. The inquest was adjourned and we heard no more from Roger.

"No, he hasn't said anything to Jack or me," Rosemary said, as we worked peacefully together in her greenhouse, potting up some spare plants for the Help the Aged coffee morning. "But then he wouldn't, not about a case he's working on. And no," she added, "I'm quite sure he doesn't think you or Michael are murderers."

"Sorry to go on about it," I said apologetically, "but we are the only people Graham knew down here."

"People do get from A to B in motorcars," Rosemary said. "They do it all the time."

"Yes, well . . ."

"Nothing to stop that nephew of his whizzing down the motorway, doing the deadly deed, and whizzing back again. *Has* he got an alibi?"

"I don't know," I replied. "They were both out when I rang later that day—at least the answerphone was on. I assumed they were at work."

"Horrid things, answerphones," Rosemary said. "I never leave messages on them. My mind simply freezes up when they give that nasty little bleep and I can't say a word. And I always bitterly resent the fact that *I've* had to pay for the call when there's no one there!"

"I suppose Roger's checked Clive's alibi by now," I said. "And his wife's, too, come to think of it. If the motive was Graham's money, she'd have just as much to gain—they might have been in it together."

"I'm sure money's much the strongest motive for murder," Rosemary said, scattering some Perlite in the general direction of a pot she'd filled. "So they must be the prime suspects."

"You're probably right," I agreed.

"There now, that's the last one." Rosemary dusted the compost off her hands. "Let's go and have some coffee. Are you going to the garden party at Chillington?"

"Yes, rather. It's very good of Josh to open up the house and grounds like this. He's such a private person, it must be disagreeable for him."

"Well, it is for a special cause," Rosemary said. "The hospice, I mean. I suppose he wants to do it because of Alison."

Alison was Josh's wife, who had spent some months in the hospice before she died of cancer last year.

I sighed. "Poor Josh, he's been so marvelous about it all. They were so devoted. If only there'd been children—now he's all alone. Oh, I know he's got masses of friends, but it's not the same. It's so dreadfully sad."

Joshua Brendon had been a client of my husband, Peter, and had, over the years, become a friend. He is the owner of Chillington Hall, which he had inherited at an early age when his parents were killed in an accident abroad. He was a golden boy—rich, handsome, and talented—for whom everything seemed so easy. When he was still at Oxford he had gathered around him a circle of equally charismatic people and had made Chillington a center for social and artistic brilliance. He has considerable musical gifts and was a successful and well-known composer of music for films and television. Yet, with all this—the success and the glamour—he is the sweetest-natured person, kind and generous, a loyal and loving friend, quite unspoiled by wealth or success. He had been very lucky to find Alison, just such another lovable person, and they had been so happy together.

"I hope this fine weather will hold," Rosemary said. "I know they're going to have the refreshments in the Great Hall if it rains, but people are far more likely to turn out on a nice day when they can poke about the grounds."

It *was* a nice day, the first really warm one we'd had, so I was able to wear my new summer frock.

On an impulse I added a wide-brimmed straw hat and I was glad I'd done so, since the first person I saw when I got to Chillington was Mrs. Dudley, Rosemary's mother, a formidable old lady with strong views on absolutely everything.

"Ah, Sheila!" She was, as usual, holding court, seated on an ornate garden chair set under the large and handsome cedar tree that shaded the lawn. I went dutifully toward her. "I am glad to see that you, at least, know what is fitting. I cannot imagine how I came to have a daughter who sees nothing wrong in appearing in public looking like a gypsy!" She gestured toward Rosemary, who was standing behind her wearing a perfectly respectable cream linen suit. Rosemary made a face at me behind her mother's back and said, "Oh, Mother, you know hats always give me a headache!"

Mrs. Dudley motioned me toward a chair beside her, and I sat down reluctantly.

"I'll just go and get you some tea," Rosemary said hastily and made her escape.

"Quite a good number of people here," I said.

"A lot of riff-raff," Mrs. Dudley said dismissively. "Hardly anyone I know. Why Joshua invited some of them I cannot think." Mrs. Dudley had obviously chosen to imagine that this was a private party for selected guests. She regarded with some distaste a young woman in jeans, sneakers, and a petrol station T-shirt. "I can well imagine what Viola Brendon would have said to all this!"

Mrs. Dudley hadn't been personally acquainted

with Josh's parents, but a little thing like that would certainly not stop her from attributing thoughts to them.

"Josh is doing it for charity," I said, "so the more the merrier, really."

She regarded me coldly. "I always think that charity begins at home," she said. This remark, although not in itself relevant, silenced me and Mrs. Dudley continued. "Chillington has been in the Brendon family for over two hundred years. It is a tragedy to think that there is no heir."

"Well, there is an heir," I said. "I mean, if Josh doesn't marry again and have a son. There's a cousin who lives in Wales, I believe."

"Wales!" Mrs. Dudley exclaimed in her most formidable Lady Bracknell tones. "What on earth is he doing in Wales?"

"I think he's got some sort of farm. Peter and I met him once, he seemed very nice."

"A farmer! Hardly the sort of person to inherit all this!"

Certainly Chillington Hall is very beautiful. It is a fine eighteenth-century house of mellow brick with two wings, or pavilions, as I think they're called, at either end. A wide terrace leads down, by way of a great sweep of curving steps, to the lawn on which we now sat, and the grounds stretch away as far as the eye can see to handsomely laid-out parkland, dotted with fine old trees and the glint of a lake in the distance. A perfect setting, a glorious example of English landscaping at its best.

"It is beautiful," I agreed. "And it's really looking heavenly at this time of the year. Aren't those rhododendrons magnificent! Josh is very lucky to have the staff to keep it up so splendidly. I suppose he must make a lot of money from his music."

"The Brendon money has always come from investments, although there are, of course, several farms and quite a lot of land. But William Brendon—that is, Joshua's grandfather—made his fortune in South Africa. Diamonds, I think, or possibly gold."

Mrs. Dudley always knew about things like that.

"Goodness, how fascinating! Well, only that sort of money can keep somewhere like this going nowadays, without opening it to the public or giving it to the National Trust."

"A dreadful state of affairs . . ."

Mrs. Dudley's familiar diatribe against present-day living was mercifully interrupted by the return of Rosemary with a tray. While she was criticizing her daughter's choice of refreshments, I made my escape.

I went up the steps onto the terrace and was just making my selection from the splendid array of food laid out when a voice behind me said, "Old Josh certainly does these things jolly well."

It was Paul Heywood.

"Paul! How nice to see you. Is Alice with you?"

"No, one of the goats is farrowing, or whatever goats do, so she wouldn't come."

I wasn't surprised to see that he'd piled a number

of small sandwiches onto his plate as well as quite a few cakes, since I knew from experience that Alice's cooking was decidedly sketchy. I made a more modest selection and we moved away to the end of the terrace.

"Well," Paul said, resting his laden plate on the wide stone balustrade, "how's everything? It must have been a dreadful shock, poor old Graham being mugged!"

"I'm afraid it's even worse than that," I said. "He wasn't mugged." I told him about the finding of the wallet. "So you see, it seems to have been a deliberate murder."

"Murder!" His hand jerked and a couple of sandwiches fell off his plate onto the ground. "You can't be serious! Is that what the police really think?"

"Yes, I'm afraid so."

"But who . . . I mean, the only people he knew in Taviscombe were you and Michael. You can't mean they suspect *you*?"

"No," I said, "I don't think they do. Well, you know how Graham always told everyone about his every move—so, more or less all his acquaintance would have known that he walked by the sea before breakfast."

"I have heard him mention it, on several occasions," Paul said with heavy irony. "So you think someone might have tracked him down to Taviscombe. But why there? Why not in London?"

"It would be a bit trickier to get him in Hyde Park," I suggested. "More people about. Anyway, perhaps whoever it was thought it would divert suspicion if the murder happened far away."

"Yes, that's true. *Have* the police any idea who might have done it?"

"I don't think so—it's early days yet. They've only just found the wallet."

Paul bent down and picked up the fallen sandwiches. "So," he said, "they haven't any clue to what the motive might have been?"

"Not as far as I know. What *could* it have been? Graham wasn't the sort of person to make that sort of enemy—I mean, he used to irritate us all quite dreadfully, I know, but that isn't a motive for murder. And he led such a blameless—you might say boring—life so there couldn't be anything there."

Paul finished off the last of the cakes, looked regretfully at the two rather dusty sandwiches, and put the plate aside.

"He must have been worth quite a bit," he said. "I suppose the nephew, what's his name, will inherit?"

"Presumably. Graham was fond of him, I think; at least he was always going on about him and how marvelous he was."

"Well, there you are, then."

"Yes, well, it is a motive, I agree, but . . ."

"For all we know, this nephew may be in all sorts of financial trouble and desperate for some extra cash," Paul said, warming to his theme. "He's something in the City, isn't he? Probably one of those Lloyds names, or whatever they're called—a lot of those people are staring ruin in the face!"

"Well, I daresay the police will be going into all that," I said. "Alibis and all that sort of thing." I really didn't feel like speculating anymore about Graham's death; I just wanted a peaceful day out away from it all.

"Isn't it a glorious day!" I said, trying to change the subject. "Perfect weather for this sort of occasion."

Paul laughed. "Chillington weather," he said, "that's what we used to call it."

I looked at him enquiringly.

"When we used to come down with Josh for the Long Vacation." Paul and Bryan and Alec had been up at Oxford with Josh, all part of the Brendon circle. "Those were marvelous days." Paul's voice softened as he remembered. "The feeling of everything being new and exciting, wonderful and extraordinary things to do—books and music to be written, plays to be performed; we felt we could achieve anything we wanted, the world was at our feet! It was such a golden time—the very air around us seemed to glitter!" He spread his arms wide in an expansive gesture. "I don't think it was just because we were young. I think we really had something special. It was Josh, of course, he held the whole thing together in his own two hands." Paul sighed. "We'll never see anything like it again, I don't suppose. People, young people now, don't seem to have that mixture of creativity, frivolity, and—oh, I suppose you could call it *style*. The end of an era. *'Tout passe, tout lasse, tout casse . . .'*"

" '*L'amitié reste,*' " I concluded the quotation. "You're still friends, you and Josh and Bryan and Alec. And you've all been successful in your own particular way. You've all fulfilled your early promise. That's something, surely?"

Paul laughed. "Yes, of course, you're right, as always, Sheila. I was just indulging in middle-aged melancholy. We've all done very well and we're the lucky ones, to have such memories."

A wood pigeon flew down onto the balustrade and began eyeing Paul's plate hopefully. Paul picked up the sandwiches and crumbled them into small pieces, throwing them onto the terrace for the bird to peck at.

"Did Graham ever come to Chillington?" I asked idly.

Paul threw the last crust toward the pigeon and brushed the crumbs from his hand. "A few times," he said. "You know how he'd always trail along behind us all. And he was up at Oxford with the rest of us, so he got included in the general invitation."

"Just a few times?"

"Yes, but it wasn't really his scene. And I somehow got the impression that Josh didn't take to him. Oh, he was always polite and welcoming—that's Josh's way—but I don't think they were ever on the same wavelength."

"No," I said, "I don't suppose they would be. Anyway, as you say, Graham wouldn't really have fitted into the Chillington circle."

The pigeon, having finished its repast, flew up

onto the balustrade, where it sat making loud crooning sounds. I picked up my empty plate.

"I'll just get rid of this and then I must go and find Josh. I haven't seen him yet and I'd like to say hello. I'll leave you with your noisy companion."

I found Josh talking to one of the hospice workers, whom I knew slightly.

"Hello, Josh, hello, Freda. What a splendid day it's been. Marvelous organization, Josh, well done!"

"Oh, Freda and Evelyn did all the work, I just stood by and admired!" Josh gave me his warm, open smile. "Lovely to see you, Sheila. Don't you look smart! That shade of blue suits you!"

"Do forgive me!" Freda waved the clipboard she was carrying. "I must just go and check with Maureen that *both* the leaflets were put out in the Great Hall. I'll see you later, Josh. Nice to have seen you, Sheila—you are coming to our sixty/forty auction next month, aren't you?"

"Yes, of course," I said meekly.

"A marvelous woman," Josh said, as she disappeared briskly in the direction of the house. "A human dynamo! Always on the go. I don't think I've ever seen her stay in one place for more than five minutes at a time!"

"Marvelous," I echoed, "but exhausting. She does so much! People like Freda always make me feel so inadequate."

"Nonsense, Sheila, you're full of good works."

"Oh, dear, that sounds like some dismal Victorian matron!"

Josh laughed. "Stop fishing for compliments, dear, you know perfectly well what I mean."

I smiled back at him, as one always does with Josh. "Well, you've certainly done the hospice proud today."

"Yes, it's been a good turnout." He paused and then said tentatively, "I was sorry to hear about Graham. It must have been—must be—very distressing for you to have to cope with all that. What happened, exactly?"

I gave him a brief summary of events and he listened intently.

"And do the police have any idea of who might . . . ?"

"Not to my knowledge," I said. "But they've really only just begun to investigate it as murder and not just a particularly brutal robbery."

"Of course, Graham wasn't a very close friend, but we've known each other for some years and, well, it was such a shocking thing to have happened!"

"Yes," I said, "it has been rather awful."

"Horrible for you," he said sympathetically. "All the enquiries and everything."

"It is. And so *inexplicable*, too. I've been racking my brains, but I simply can't think of any reason why Graham should have been killed like that."

"Sheila," Josh began, "I want to talk to you. Not here," he added as several admirers made as if to approach him. "Let's go across to the studio. We won't be disturbed there."

I was curious to know what Josh might have to say that needed privacy and followed as he moved quickly across the lawns and made his way back toward the house and the old stables that he had turned into a studio. It was pleasantly cool in the stable yard after the heat of the gardens. Josh unlocked the door and we went in.

"It's a bit stuffy in here," he said. "I'll leave the door open for a bit to let a little air in."

I'd never been into Josh's studio before, and for a moment I stood in the doorway completely taken aback by the extraordinary contrast of the high-tech equipment and the building that contained it. The old stalls still remained, with their elegantly carved wooden finials and the wrought iron mangers for the hay, as did the original floor with the herring-bone pattern of brick. But inside the stalls there was built-in shelving and cupboards, stacked with equipment whose function I couldn't even guess at, and handsome Afghan rugs were scattered over the floor.

"Goodness," I said, "Grinling Gibbons meets Starship *Enterprise*!"

Josh laughed. "Yes, it is a bit bizarre at first glance," he said. "But it's an ideal place—well away from the house, nice thick eighteenth-century walls—perfect. Let's have a little light."

He switched on a couple of spotlights, and I looked about me in bewilderment.

"What on earth *is* everything?" I asked. "I mean, I assume that's a keyboard, and that looks like some sort of monitor, but after that—well!"

Josh waved his hand in the general direction of what looked to me like a pile of video players one on top of the other. "That's a Jo Meek Compresser, that's a Quadraverb, that's a Lexicon Reverb and an Alesis Reverb. Now over *here*"—indicating a large object with plugs and wires sticking out of it—"we have the mixing desk, the keyboard is a Korg, by the way, and the sound modules are over here." He gestured toward another bank of black machines with little knobs and things. "That's a Proteus 1—that's band—and Proteus 2—that's orchestra, the Procussion drum machine, and the Yamaha RMSO drum machine, there's the wavestation, and down at the bottom are the sound samplers, and the optical disk is at the top there . . ." He broke off and laughed as he saw the expression on my face. "Well, you *did* ask," he said.

"It must have cost a fortune!"

"About forty thousand pounds basic and whatever you like for the extras."

"Goodness!"

"Yes, well, tools of the trade, as it were. Anyway, I didn't bring you in here to bore you with my enthusiasms. Do sit down. I wanted a word—I was going to ring you, actually, if I hadn't seen you today—but it's probably better not to say this over the phone."

"That sounds very mysterious."

"Well, it's something I think you—and the police, too, if you think it's necessary—ought to know."

Josh's face, usually smiling and relaxed, looked serious, almost stern.

"Josh, what do you mean? What is it?"

"It's about Graham. Something I found out—I think you should know—" He broke off as a figure appeared in the open doorway. It was Mrs. Dudley.

"Ah, Sheila," she said, "I thought I saw you coming in here. Rosemary seems to have disappeared and I would like to go home now. Perhaps you would be good enough to drive me back to Taviscombe."

· 6 ·

Josh's exclamation of annoyance was so unlike him that even Mrs. Dudley was taken aback.

"I do apologize," she said, her beady eyes resting upon us, bright with curiosity. "I do hope I'm not interrupting anything important."

Josh recollected himself and smiled politely. "No, not at all," he said.

"It's the sun," Mrs. Dudley continued, "so strong. I was afraid if I stayed any longer it might bring on one of my heads. I cannot *think* where Rosemary has gone. I've looked everywhere for her."

She looked me straight in the eye, daring me to contradict her. We both knew that her search for Rosemary would have been perfunctory and that she had simply used her as an excuse to follow me and poke about in a part of the house she hadn't seen before. I knew I was right when she looked about her and said, "So this is where you write all that music. How interesting. And what," she asked, pointing with her stick to the mixing desk, "is that?"

Josh gave her a modified version of the explanation he had given me, but she wasn't really listening, her gaze searching for something more personal that she could relate to (and, if possible, disapprove of) in this wilderness of technology.

"Most interesting," she repeated. "And to think," she added with her customary acerbity, "that Beethoven managed to write all those symphonies and concertos without the benefit of all *this!*"

Josh gave a polite laugh, and Mrs. Dudley, having satisfied her curiosity and garnered enough information to impress her cronies ("Oh, yes, such a great friend, he showed me the studio where he composes—most impressive . . .") turned to me.

"Very well, then, Sheila, if you're ready."

Behind her back, Josh gave me a resigned shrug. "I'll be in touch, Sheila," he said. "I've got to go to New York for a week or two, but I'll ring you when I'm back and you must come to lunch."

"Lovely," I said, "I'll look forward to that. Good-bye, Josh, have a good trip."

All the way home I was consumed with curiosity as to what it was that Josh had been going to tell me. Beside me in the car, Mrs. Dudley kept up a running commentary on the events of the afternoon.

"The food really was quite good—did you have any of that lemon cake?—but only Indian tea, no Earl Grey. You would have thought that Joshua might have seen to that, though I suppose Freda Martock arranged that side and I don't suppose she has any idea of how things should be done. Poor Joshua, I thought he looked very strained. I don't suppose he will ever get over losing Alison. Such a charming girl—her aunt was a second cousin of mine. Did you not know that? Oh, yes . . ."

The voice went on relentlessly while I turned over and over in my mind what on earth Josh thought I ought to know about Graham. And the police, too. That sounded serious. And now, because Josh was going to be away, I wouldn't know for several weeks. It was all deeply frustrating, and I was furious with Mrs. Dudley for interrupting when she did.

Rosemary rang the next morning full of apologies.

"I'm frightfully sorry about Mother! Needless to say I was waiting around to take her home and couldn't find her. Fortunately Josh told me that she'd hijacked you, else I'd have been waiting still!"

"Oh, that's all right," I said. "It didn't matter."

"She really is quite impossible!" Rosemary paused for a moment and then said tentatively, "Mother said that you and Josh were having a cosy tête-à-tête in the old stables. I do hope she didn't barge in on anything important."

"No, not really," I said. "He just wanted to have a chat, and you know how difficult that is when you're surrounded by people all wanting to ask something." For some reason I didn't feel I could tell anyone what Josh wanted to talk about.

"Oh, well, that's all right then, as long as it wasn't anything special. It was a really good show yesterday, wasn't it? They must have raised a fabulous amount of money for the hospice. And how lucky it was such a lovely day."

"Chillington weather," I said absently.

"What?"

"Oh, just something Paul Heywood said yesterday. He was remembering that time in the sixties when Josh used to hold court—a golden age, he called it."

"Mm, yes," Rosemary said. "It always sounded so glamorous! A sort of cross between Brideshead and Garsington! All those talented, charismatic people. Don't you wish we'd been a part of it?"

"I don't know. Perhaps as a fly on the wall. Fascinating to have observed it all."

"There's something about Josh," Rosemary went on, "there always has been, something special. Not just that he's such a thoroughly nice person, not to mention rich and good-looking, but a quality—I don't know what—that's, well, as I said, special."

"I think perhaps it's that he brings out the best in people. In lots of ways. Not just basic things like good manners, but he makes you feel that any talent you have for anything, however small, is worthwhile and important. I know that, when I've been with him, I always feel I want to go away and do something *splendid*—write a brilliant analysis of *The*

Golden Bowl, a definitive life of Jane Austen, nothing seems beyond my capabilities! The effect soon wears off, of course, and I go back to recognizing my limitations, but it does make you realize what sort of effect he must have had on really creative people."

"Goodness! Yes." Rosemary seemed a little taken aback by my burst of enthusiasm. "You're right, of course. He was a terrific influence. Anyway, on a more prosaic level, he certainly did a lot yesterday for good causes. Which reminds me, I hate to ask, but do you think you could make a couple of Victoria sponges for the coffee morning next week? I did ask Estelle, but she's got her grandchildren for the week—it's half-term—five of them, just imagine! So she can't cope with anything else."

I felt I really must do something about clearing up the spare room. Roger had said that he didn't need to look through Graham's things again so I rang up Clive and asked him what he wanted me to do with them.

"Well, if you *could* send them on to me," Clive said, "I would be most grateful. I had intended to come down to Taviscombe myself, but I have to be in Frankfurt for a few days. . . . However, the police have now released the body so I have arranged the funeral for next week, Friday. I do hope you will be able to come. I know it would have meant so much to Uncle Graham to have all his friends there. I always thought he had such a talent for friendship."

I didn't feel that I could comment on this statement, so I said briefly that of course I would be at the funeral.

"Angela will send you details," he said fussily in a way that reminded me of Graham. "The time and how to get to the church and so forth."

"Actually," I said, "I could bring Graham's things with me then. They're all in his suitcase, of course, and it would be easier to cope with it that way than try and parcel it all up!"

"Yes, of course, if it isn't too much trouble, that would be excellent. Actually, I have to be in London on the Thursday, why don't we meet at Uncle Graham's flat and you could bring them there. That might be more convenient."

"Oh, yes," I said thankfully, since the thought of lugging a heavy suitcase all the way to Gerrards Cross hadn't been appealing. "That would be splendid. I shall be staying at my club in South Audley Street and that's quite near."

"Really?" Clive seemed impressed with the location and, perhaps on the strength of that, added, "Let us say twelve-thirty, and then we might have lunch. There is quite a tolerable little Italian place just round the corner from there."

Relieved that that particular problem was settled, I went upstairs to the spare room, having taken the precaution of shutting Foss up in the kitchen, since anything to do with making or unmaking beds always has his enthusiastic and unhelpful cooperation. I took off the duvet cover and the pillowcases and I was just untucking the undersheet when it got caught in the casters of the bed. I moved it to one side and, in doing so, revealed a document that had got pushed out of sight under the bed. Presumably Graham had been doing a little bedside reading and one of the papers had slipped out of the file. I stooped to pick it up and took it over to the window to examine it more closely.

It was a copy of a letter from Graham to Paul Heywood.

Dear Paul,

I have noted the points you made in your letter of the 14th, and after careful consideration, I do feel that I must advise you to continue with the appeal. We do have a very strong chance of winning and it would be foolish to abandon the case now, especially in view of the costs already involved.

Furthermore, I am sure I do not have to remind you of the long-standing obligation involved, which would make the continuance of the case imperative.

I shall look forward to hearing from you at your earliest convenience, since it will be necessary to move as quickly as possible in this matter.

Yours sincerely,

Feeling, rather guiltily, that I shouldn't have read it, I put the letter back into the folder with the others.

Now it would be up to Graham's partners to decide whether or not to encourage Paul to go on with the dispute. I put the folders away in the suitcase and closed it up. I really would be very glad to get it out of the house, since it was a palpable reminder of the horrible thing that had happened and, in some obscure way, a reproach as well.

"Are you sure you don't mind my not coming to the funeral?" Michael asked. "I do feel rather mean leaving you to face it by yourself. But we've got this complicated case coming up next week and I really ought to be in court with Edward."

"No, it's fine, really. Anyway, I won't be alone—Paul and probably Bryan will be there, too. And I do want to spend a day in the British Library—I've got a few things I need to check—and then Richard Allbright wants to see me about those reviews. . . . To be honest, you'll be far more use, from my point of view, staying at home looking after the animals!"

Since the weather was unexpectedly hot, I was glad that I had managed to get a room at the club at the back, overlooking the little garden, away from the heat and traffic noise of South Audley Street. I opened the window and looked with pleasure at the great plane tree, taller even than the high Victorian house itself, that grew in the garden, and at the white-painted chairs and tables that stood in its shade. It would have been pleasant simply to sit out there with a coffee and the morning paper, as several of the members were doing, rather than having to lug Graham's suitcase along to his Bayswater flat and talk to his rather tiresome-sounding nephew. Still, I was curious to know what sort of person Clive was. After all, as Michael had said, he was the person who would benefit most from Graham's death. The prime suspect, in fact. I wondered if he had an alibi and how I could maneuver the conversation round so that I could somehow ask him about it.

It was still rather early, but I wasn't sure how long it would take me to find a taxi, so I thought I'd go at once. I took the rackety little lift downstairs, and by a fortunate chance a taxi was pulling up outside the club, depositing an elderly member, so I got one straight away and arrived at Graham's flat almost a whole hour before I was due to meet Clive. It was in a block of Edwardian mansion flats, and the front hall was spacious and decorated in the style of the period, with a lot of gilt-framed mirrors and heavy velvet hangings. The porter at the desk was an elderly man, also old-fashioned in his politeness and concern that I would have to wait so long.

"Mrs. Malory? Yes, Mr. Merivale did phone through to say that he would be meeting you here at twelve-thirty. I'm very sorry you will have such a long time to wait."

"It's my own fault," I said, "I'm always early for everything."

He smiled politely at my remark and then went on. "We were all very sorry to hear about Mr. Percy," he said. "It was a dreadful thing. We were all quite shocked when we heard about it. Such a quiet gentleman—a little, what shall I say, *pernickety* on occasion, but very quiet at all times. And he was a friend of yours?"

"Yes," I said, "he was staying with me when the—the sad event occurred. That's why I'm here. To return his suitcase to Mr. Merivale."

The porter shook his head. "That must have been a terrible shock for you, to have such a thing happen to an old friend."

"Yes, it was very distressing."

We were both silent for a moment as if in acknowledgment of the distress.

The porter leaned forward confidentially. "I'm afraid it's not very comfortable down here in the hall in this hot weather," he said apologetically. "We normally have air conditioning, but it's not working properly—typical, isn't it, in the only hot weather we've had this year!—and I can't leave the main door open, I'm afraid, because of the security, you see." He came out from behind the desk and indicated an area with a chair, a small table, and a large potted palm. "Perhaps you'd like to take a seat over here."

I thanked him and sat down.

It really was very hot and stuffy, and I thought longingly of my own cool garden at home. The minutes ticked by, and I cursed myself for not having brought a book.

After about five minutes the porter came over.

"I was thinking. Since you are such an old friend

of Mr. Percy, I'm sure he wouldn't mind—wouldn't have minded—you going up to his flat and waiting there. It would be much cooler."

I got up with alacrity. "Oh, could I? That would be marvelous. It really is very close in here." I tried to look like the sort of person who might quite possibly faint if overcome by excessive heat. "And I'm sure Mr. Merivale would have no objection in the circumstances."

In acknowledgment of this, the porter picked up the suitcase and led the way to the lift. Graham's flat was on the second floor. The porter took out his pass key and opened the door.

"The cleaner was in this morning," he said, "so she'll have opened the windows and given everything a good airing."

"Oh, yes," I said gratefully, "it's *much* cooler up here!"

When the porter had gone I looked around me. I had been to the flat with Peter some years before, and I saw that my memory of the drawing room as a dark, unwelcoming place had not been wrong. The walls were covered in some sort of porridge-like paper, and the prevailing color scheme was fawn and brown. The furniture was heavy and solid, the curtains a depressing shade of mustard. There was an old-fashioned standard lamp with a fringed shade, and on the wall a series of engravings of Oxford colleges.

I sat down in an uncomfortable large leather armchair and looked at a photograph on the table beside it. It was of Dulcie and her husband, Arthur. I picked it up and studied it. There was a definite family resemblance between Dulcie and her brother. She, too, had that dark wiry hair that always makes me think of a terrier, the same sort of nose (the Percy nose, Graham affirmed with pride), and the same dark eyes, though hers were larger and more reproachful. I remember thinking, on the few occasions I'd met her, that she was the sort of woman who always has to have some sort of grievance, some cause for complaint. Which probably explained why her husband, in the photograph at any rate (I never actually met him), had such an apologetic air, obviously having been held responsible for all her real or fancied ills.

I got up and prowled restlessly around, opening doors and peering inside. Graham's bedroom was dark and gloomy, too, containing a single bed with an old-fashioned eiderdown and two large, mahogany wardrobes and chests of drawers. It was, of course, impeccably tidy and totally characterless. The bathroom was small and spartan, and the kitchen was the typical kitchen of a bachelor who obviously never cooked for himself. Idly I opened the fridge and found only a couple of cartons of long-life milk, half a dozen eggs, and an unopened packet of processed cheese slices.

I went back into the drawing room and looked at my watch. There was still half an hour before Clive Merivale was due. I looked around for something to read, but apart from various legal books and an atlas, there was nothing. The room, I decided, really was like something caught up in a time warp. Even the television set was small and obviously an early model. In fact the only modern object in the room was an answerphone.

Once I had taken in its presence, my eye kept being drawn back to it, rather as if in a film the camera had focused on it to make some significant point. I crossed the room toward it, and without allowing myself to think what I was doing, I pressed the button marked "Messages." There was a short silence, then a voice that I recognized as Paul Heywood's.

"Graham, look, things are getting out of hand. Please ring me."

There was a bleep to mark the end of the message, then a short pause, then the same voice.

"Graham! Didn't you get my message—you said you'd check your answerphone while you were away—you know I can't ring you about this at Sheila's! For God's sake, ring me!"

Another bleep, then another voice, also familiar, the tone less desperate, more sardonic.

"Graham? I refer you to Section 36 of the Trustee Act 1925, and I'll see you in hell first!"

There was a final bleep and then a click as the machine turned itself off.

· 7 ·

The voice of the second caller hovered infuriatingly around the edges of my mind for several minutes until I finally pinned it down. It was Bryan Shelley. Now I was really puzzled. The mounting hysteria of Paul's calls was strange enough, but combined with Bryan's message, it opened up several avenues of speculation.

I had no time, however, to embark on any sort of conjecture since, at that moment, I heard the lift doors close and footsteps in the corridor outside. I moved hastily away from the answerphone, and as I heard the sound of the key in the door, I settled myself in the depths of the leather armchair, trying to look as if I had been sitting there for the last half hour. I was praying, too, that the answerphone wouldn't do anything awkward like rewinding and repeating the messages so that it would be obvious that I'd been fiddling with it.

The door opened and a tall, thick-set man came

in. I got up from the chair and went forward to greet him.

"Clive? I'm Sheila Malory." We shook hands formally and I went on, "I do hope you didn't mind my waiting up here—the porter suggested it because it was so *dreadfully* hot down in the hall."

I burbled on, consciously trying to disarm him, trying to give the impression of the rather feather-headed female that I calculated he would respond to.

"No, of course not," he said smoothly. "I really am most grateful to you for bringing Uncle's things up to London. I do hope it wasn't too much of a bother."

Clive Merivale didn't look like his uncle at all. For that matter, he didn't look like his mother or father, either. What he did look like was one of those bland, sleek villains in 1930s gangster movies—a sort of George Raft type—even down to the slicked-back dark hair and the small moustache. I was so taken with this resemblance that I didn't listen very carefully to what he was saying until the name Paul Heywood focused my attention.

"Paul?"

"Yes," Clive said. "He rang me yesterday and suggested that, since he was coming for the funeral, he might drive over and collect Uncle's case from you to save you the bother of bringing it with you. But, of course, you'd already left by then."

"Did he! That was considerate of him."

What could Paul have wanted from Graham's

case? I looked at the suitcase standing forlornly in the center of the room. The document file, presumably. But why?

Clive was telling me about the funeral arrangements and listing with tedious thoroughness the times of the trains from Marylebone to Gerrards Cross that I had already looked up for myself.

"Right, then," he said briskly. "Let's go and get some lunch. This flat always gives me the willies—so dismal!" He looked around at the depressing furnishings. "I used to dread coming here when I was a boy and Mother used to bring me to see Uncle Graham. Even though he used to give me a quid when we left—'To buy an ice cream.' He always used to say that." He laughed, and I was suddenly touched at the thought of Graham, awkwardly confronted with a small child, trying to establish some sort of contact with what must have been, to him, a totally alien creature.

"It's a bit as though it's been preserved in aspic," I said. "1940s—well, 1930s really, or even '20s. I imagine most of the furniture was his parents'."

"Yes. No sort of market for all this large stuff now, nobody's got the room. That lamp, though, and the clock and that mirror"—he turned to examine them with more interest—"they might fetch something—Art Deco's quite collectible, I believe."

I didn't say anything. I felt uncomfortable, hearing him calculating the possible commercial value of his uncle's possessions.

"I suppose I'd better let Angela have a look to see

if there's anything she wants, but I wouldn't think so. We've got modern stuff—Scandinavian—none of this would fit." He went over to the window, raised the Venetian blind, and looked out. "It's not a bad position, this flat, what you might call the better end of Bayswater. Uncle Graham bought it years ago, when prices were quite low, but it was a ninety-nine-year lease, and there's still a good bit to run. So, even with house prices as they are now, he was sitting on a little gold mine—I often told him so. 'If you sold this place tomorrow,' I said, 'you'd make a tidy packet!' Well, I suppose I'd better see about putting it on the market. There's no point in letting it stand empty."

He spoke as if it was certain that he would inherit from his uncle. Perhaps it was. Graham might have told him so. In fact, he may very well have used the bait of the inheritance as a means of keeping Clive dancing attendance. From what I knew of Graham and what I'd now seen of Clive, this seemed more than likely.

"Well, lunch it is, then. I'll come back and pick up the case afterwards."

The little Italian place was, as I'd expected, really quite grand, with the full complement of obsequious waiters and an excessively expensive wine list.

"Now then," Clive said, leaning toward me attentively, "what are you going to have? They do a rather interesting thing here with polenta and wild mushrooms."

I declined the proffered treat. It may be fashionable, but polenta, however interestingly done, always reminds me somehow of the overcooked semolina pudding of my schooldays, while I find the term "wild" as applied to food ("wild mushrooms," "wild rabbit") pretentious and off-putting. I chose the chicken in Madeira and elected to drink mineral water.

"One of the tiresome things about middle age," I said, "is that even a small amount of alcohol at midday makes one intolerably sleepy all afternoon."

We chatted lightly for a while—at least, Clive told me, in the sort of boring detail that brought his uncle vividly to mind, about his travels in Europe and how he had "put one over" (his phrase) on assorted businessmen in France, Germany, and the Benelux countries.

In a brief pause, while the waiter was pouring him another glass of wine, I said, "I was so sorry I couldn't get through to you straight away when your uncle died, but, of course, with you and Angela both working . . ."

"Yes, and that was the day when Greta—that's the au pair—wasn't there either, because she had to take Junior to the dentist. We've got this marvelous man in Harley Street, but, of course, it means the best part of a day getting up to Town and back. No, Angela was at her office, and I didn't get back—I'd been to Leeds for a couple for days—until that evening."

"Quite a long journey," I said sympathetically. "If you drove, that is. Or did you do it by train?"

For some reason he hesitated, then replied, "Oh, car, of course. I don't like to be tied down to train timetables when I've got a deal on."

"I'm not mad about trains myself," I said, "but the motorways are so awful now, all those heavy lorries! And the parking! Were you staying in the center of Leeds? Peter and I stayed at the Queen's the one time we were there, and my friend Rosemary tells me that there's a marvelous place in the Calles—is that what they're called?"

"Actually," he said, "I wasn't in Leeds all the time. I had people to see in Sheffield and Nottingham . . ." He drank some of the wine.

I had the feeling that he was being evasive and I wondered why. He began to talk about Graham.

"A funny sort of chap, really. Never married. Nowadays people would think all sorts of things!"

"A bachelor," I said. "A born bachelor, even. The term has quite gone now. Like spinster. It's funny really how things can change so radically in such a short space of time."

Clive poured the rest of the wine into his glass. "I've been in touch with his firm, of course. They were all very shocked. He was a partner, you know, and had some very important clients."

"Yes," I said, "I know. Oh, by the way, he had a

couple of files with him—I packed them with the other things in his suitcase."

Clive laughed. "Good old Uncle Graham," he said, "always combining business with pleasure! Never missed an opportunity. I'll take them round to his office. There are a few things I'll need to see them about, you understand, in connection with the estate. Now then, what about a pudding? The zabaglione's very good here."

I shook my head. "No, really, just coffee would be fine."

"Well, I think I'll have the profiteroles—are you sure you won't join me?" He gave the order to the waiter and leaned forward confidentially. "So what do the police think? Have they got any sort of clue, any idea who might have done it?"

"I don't think so. I've certainly heard nothing."

"I still think it was some young hooligan trying to rob him. That's the only explanation that makes any sense."

"But they found the wallet with the money and credit cards still in it."

"Well, he could have dropped it, run away in a panic when he saw what he'd done, the wallet could have fallen in the sea."

"The tide was out," I said.

"Well, onto the beach then," he said impatiently, "and then got washed out with the tide and washed in again. I mean, all this far-fetched nonsense about someone tracking him down to Taviscombe and murdering him. And for what possible reason? I ask you! You knew Uncle Graham. Was he the sort of person anyone would want to murder?"

"Well, no . . ."

"Exactly. All a lot of nonsense. These dropouts and Hells Angels—you get a lot of types like that in seaside towns—that's where they should be looking." He vigorously spooned up the remaining chocolate sauce on his plate. "Now you must agree, Sheila, that makes a damned sight more sense."

"It would certainly simplify matters," I said.

The funeral was like so many funerals today. Formal and impersonal—the officiating clergyman, not having known the deceased, making some unexceptional, bland remarks. There was one wreath, of white chrysanthemums, on the coffin ("Donations to Christian Aid"), and we sang "Through All the Changing Scenes of Life" and "Guide Me, Oh Thou Great Redeemer" and the 23rd Psalm, familiar and comforting—though there was no one in that congregation, it seemed to me, who needed to be comforted.

Outside, in the warm sunshine, Clive marshaled us from the church across the green to his house, which was only a short distance away. Apart from myself and Clive and Angela, there were only Paul Heywood, Bryan Shelley, and an elderly man, wearing what I always used to think of as the uniform of the legal profession (black jacket and striped trousers), presumably a representative of Graham's firm. I noticed that Alice and Odette hadn't come, though I wasn't really surprised, since I knew that neither of them liked Graham and that his annual visits had, indeed, been the cause of marital discord for some years. However, I couldn't resist saying to Paul, who was walking beside me, "Couldn't Alice make it, then?"

"No. The goats, you know, she can't really leave them."

"Ah, yes, the goats." I probed a little more. "Clive said that you very kindly offered to collect Graham's things and bring them with you today."

Paul seemed a little disconcerted that Clive had told me.

"Yes, well, I thought it might save you the trouble."

"That was very kind of you, but it was no trouble."

"Poor old Graham. It seems funny to think he's gone. Not a bad turnout."

"What a pity Sir Alec couldn't be here."

"Alec?"

"Well, Graham had been to stay with you and Bryan and me. He was due to go on to Sir Alec next."

"Yes, of course."

"And, of course, you'd all known each other since you were at school together."

Paul sighed. "Yes, time really does rush by, doesn't it? Ah, we seem to have arrived."

Clive's house was everything Graham had said it was, large, handsome, and expensively furnished.

Angela took me into the bedroom to leave my coat
and tidy my hair. She, too, was large, handsome,
and expensively turned out, wearing a black and
white dress and jacket that must have cost more
than all my summer wardrobe put together. However, she seemed friendly enough.

"Poor Uncle Graham," she said, taking off her
large-brimmed black hat. "We were *terribly*
shocked—well, I told you when you phoned—such
a dreadful thing to have happened!"

"Yes, you will miss him."

"Oh, yes, of course," she said perfunctorily. She
picked up a bottle of scent from the dressing table
and applied some to her wrist. "It's so awful,
though, having the police involved, so inconvenient
and unpleasant."

"Inconvenient?"

"Oh, you know, they keep on ringing up to ask
where we *were* and things like that."

"I suppose they have to ask everyone certain
questions."

"Oh, yes," she said. "Poor you, being actually on
the spot—I expect you're sick to death of it all, with
that tiresome inspector on your doorstep the whole
time."

"Oh, Roger—Inspector Eliot—is an old friend.
Actually, he's married to my goddaughter."

"Oh, I see." Angela looked annoyed at this revelation. "Oh, well, then I expect he was different with
you. But I can't say I cared for the way he went
round checking up on us, as if we were *suspects* or

something. I mean, we've neither of us ever *been* to Tavistock!"

"Taviscombe," I said. "No, I'm sure he didn't mean to upset you, it's just normal police procedure. And it was a very nasty murder."

"Oh, yes, don't get me wrong! 'I know you've got your job to do,' I said. 'We quite understand that and we're very anxious to help you in any way we can, but it *is* unpleasant being faced with a lot of questions when you've just lost a very close relative.' Which he was. I mean, we were all the family poor Uncle Graham had. He was *devoted* to us, and, of course, he was Andrew's godfather, you know."

"Yes," I said, "he told us at the time how delighted he was that you'd asked him."

"I do think godparents are so important for a child," Angela continued. "Andrew's other godfather is Alastair Manheim, Clive's senior partner, and his godmother is Laura Benedict, who is the wife of *my* senior partner."

Andrew would certainly have access to a great deal of material advice as he grew up, the spiritual and moral virtues perhaps being left to develop naturally or not at all.

"Did Graham visit you often, then?" I asked.

Angela picked up a comb from the dressing table and made a minute adjustment to her impeccably set hair. "Oh well, you know how it is when everyone leads such busy lives. Though he did come to Andrew's last birthday party—well, we always have a little drinks party for the parents when they come to collect the infants—and he came to that."

"That was nice," I said.

Angela looked at me sharply, as if suspecting some irony on my part.

"Well then," she said briskly. "We'd better be getting down to join the others. I must just check that Greta's taken the food in. She does these splendid little open sandwiches (the Scandinavians are so good at that sort of thing)—I always serve them with drinks. I thought that would be most suitable. I mean, I don't suppose people feel like eating much at a time like this."

"Oh, no, that sounds just right!"

She seemed gratified by my approval and led the way down to the drawing room, where the others were standing around with drinks in their hands and already well into the open sandwiches.

Clive, who looked to be on his second large scotch, asked me what I'd like to drink. "I remember you saying you didn't drink at lunchtime," he said jovially, "but perhaps on this occasion . . . How about a glass of this rather good Sancerre?"

"That would be lovely."

With a glass in my hand as protective cover, I looked round the room. Clive was now in deep conversation with the elderly solicitor, no doubt questioning him about the will, while Paul had been backed up into a corner by Angela, who appeared, to judge from the snatches of conversation I could hear, to be giving him her description of the

Merivales and Graham as One Big Happy Family. Bryan was standing by the table apparently intent on making a selection from the appetizing-looking sandwiches arranged on a wooden platter.

I went over to him and we engaged in a little desultory chat, first about various friends we had in common in Oxford, then, more stiltedly, about Graham.

"Yes, well," Bryan said, "it'll feel funny not having him around."

"He's been a part of all our lives for so long," I agreed. "Yours more than mine, of course, because you go right back to schooldays. What was he like as a schoolboy?"

Bryan shrugged. "More or less what he was like as a grownup. Some people seem to be born middle-aged."

"Were you all always friends?"

"Well, you know what Graham was like—he sort of tagged along."

"Yes," I said, "he did that to Peter, too, at the College of Law."

Bryan leaned forward and picked up the platter of sandwiches.

"Are you going to have one of these? They're very good."

I took a sandwich and said, "I was just saying to Paul, what a pity Alec Patmore couldn't be here today to complete the circle."

"Oh, poor old Alec. I'm afraid he's really housebound now. I went down to see him about six months ago and he could hardly walk then. I believe he's stuck in a wheelchair permanently now."

"It's so sad, he was such a brilliant actor. I suppose he could do radio work, perhaps?"

"No, I asked him that. He's given up the whole thing. Actually, I think he's been wanting to give up for some time now."

"Really?"

"He sort of lost heart when Julia died—he's never been the same since."

Julia Marlowe and Alec Patmore had been one of *the* theatrical couples of their generation. She was beautiful, charming, and talented; he was powerful and charismatic—a perfect combination. Their Romeo and Juliet, when they were both heartbreakingly young, and their Beatrice and Benedick in later years, are still spoken of, by those fortunate enough to have seen them, as pure magic. It was, by all accounts, a stormy marriage, inevitable, really, with two such larger-than-life characters, but everyone was surprised when Julia suddenly went off with a young man some years her junior (playing Hamlet to her Gertrude). There was a divorce, but within a year she was dead, killed in a car crash. The young man was driving. He was killed also.

"It was so sad," I said. "She was so beautiful. I remember them in *The Taming of the Shrew*—the sheer chemistry between them was absolutely terrific! I couldn't believe it when they split up. I mean, they'd been together for years. It must have been

devastating for him when she went off with someone else. And then to die so soon after!"

"Poor old Alec, it seemed to change his whole
character. He used to be so outgoing and full of zest
for life, but since then . . . Of course, I don't suppose
this illness of his has helped—made him something
of a recluse. He sees some of his old friends, but
mostly he leads a very quiet life, does less than he
could do—physically, I mean."

"Yes," I said, "I rather gathered that. I spoke to
his dresser, when I telephoned to explain about
Graham, and, from what I gathered from him, Alec
Patmore leads a highly restricted life."

"Ah, yes, the estimable Penrose, he's absolutely
devoted. I can't imagine what Alec would do without him."

"In view of all this, I must say I'm rather surprised that Graham was going to stay. You must
admit that he wasn't the easiest of guests, and in a
household already revolving so strictly round one
difficult person—well!"

"Oh, you know what Graham was like. If he said
he was coming to stay, he just did!"

"Come to think of it," I laughed, "I seem to remember he did say that he 'proposed' himself!"

"Exactly. To be honest, it wasn't at all convenient
for him to stay with me this time, what with Odette
being away. I did sort of suggest that some other
time might be more convenient, but no."

"Graham never was susceptible to hints," I said,

"and it would take a brave person to say simply, 'Don't come.' I know, I've often thought of it!"

"Oh, well, as things are . . . Actually, I'm rather glad now that he did come. One last time, you know. And talking of visits, when are *you* coming to Oxford again and when are you coming to see us? Odette's back now, so just let me know when. It would be good to have a proper talk under slightly less depressing circumstances."

"That would be lovely," I said. "I'll give you a ring when I know . . ."

I broke off because I felt a light touch on my arm. I looked down and saw a small boy, about five years old.

"Hello," he said, "I'm Andrew. Would you like to come and see my guinea pig?"

I smiled. "Yes please, I'd like to very much."

He took my hand and was leading me out of the room when Angela looked up from her conversation.

"Don't let him be a nuisance," she said. "I don't know where Greta's got to. I told her to keep him out of the way."

"Not a nuisance in the least," I said. "We're going to see the guinea pig."

She pulled a face. "That wretched animal, it's all he ever thinks of! I can't think why Clive ever let him have it."

Andrew tugged urgently at my hand and we left the room.

It was nice to be outside in the fresh air and away

from all the people and complications indoors. I smiled gratefully at Andrew as he led me down to the bottom of the garden, where, beyond the apple trees and the fruit cage (the Merivales obviously had a very good gardener), a pen had been erected to house the guinea pig.

"His name's Sandy," Andrew explained, undoing the door and gently lifting the little creature out.

"Because he is," I said. "A beautiful sandy, golden color!"

"Would you like to hold him?" Andrew asked.

I held out my hands and took the animal from him and stroked the silky fur. "He's lovely," I said. "My little boy had a guinea pig, too, when he was your age."

"What was it called?"

"Humphrey."

"Why?"

"I don't really remember, I think it was just a name Michael (that's what my son's called) liked at the time."

"Has your little boy still got his guinea pig?" Andrew asked.

"My little boy's grown up now," I replied, "and the guinea pig died a long time ago. He lived for years and years," I added hastily since I saw Andrew looking anxiously at Sandy.

"Were you sad when it died?"

"Yes, we were."

"I would be sad if Sandy died."

He held out his hands. I put the guinea pig into

them and he nursed it gently. After a moment he said, "Are grown-ups sad when people die?"

"Yes, very sad."

"I thought they were, but when Uncle Graham died, Mummy said that it was a good thing."

"Oh, darling, I think you must have misunderstood. I'm sure she didn't say that."

"Yes, she did. She said it was good because now we wouldn't have to sell the house and move somewhere horrid. And we wouldn't have to get rid of Greta." He raised the guinea pig to his face and rubbed it against his cheek. "I don't want Greta to go because I like her. She's my friend. She's Sandy's friend, too."

"Do you remember your Uncle Graham?" I asked.

Andrew thought for a moment. "I think so. Sort of. But I only saw him a few times."

"Andrew!"

We both turned round as a figure approached us across the grass.

"Oh, Andrew! There you are!"

A tall girl with light brown hair and a pleasant expression came toward us.

"This is my friend Greta," Andrew explained.

I held out my hand. "I'm Sheila Malory. I was a friend of Mr. Merivale's uncle. Andrew has been very kindly showing me his guinea pig."

The girl smiled. "I hope he was no trouble."

"On the contrary, it was a pleasure."

She nodded understandingly. "Funerals are sad, yes? Sometimes it is good to be with the young."

She turned to her charge. "Come now, Andrew. Put Sandy away. We must all go in."

"Yes," I said reluctantly, "I suppose we must."

Sandy was put back into the pen and Andrew took Greta's hand.

"When your little boy was grown up," he asked, "did he have another guinea pig?"

"No," I replied. "But he has two dogs now. And I have a cat."

Andrew nodded, apparently satisfied. "When I'm grown up I shall have two dogs and two cats and a rabbit"—he broke away from Greta and danced in front of us chanting—"and a lion and an elephant and a crocodile . . ."

Greta laughed and chased him up the garden path.

I suppressed the thought that if it meant that Andrew could keep his friend Greta then perhaps Graham had not died in vain.

· 8 ·

"So you see," I said to Michael when he met me off the London train, "the Merivales do seem to be in financial difficulties. Which certainly makes Clive a hot suspect."

"But he was in Leeds," Michael protested.

"We-ell, actually, he did seem a bit shifty about that. He said that he wasn't in Leeds *all* the time he was away. I definitely got the feeling that he was trying to cloud the issue somehow. I wonder if Roger has checked his alibi."

"Perhaps you'd better ask him."

"Perhaps I will. Certainly Clive does seem to be the one who had the most to gain from Graham's death. He's a pretty unlovely sort of person, actually, and Angela's no better—worse, in some ways."

"In that case it won't upset you too much if he turns out to be a murderer."

"Not really. Except that—oh, dear, if Clive *is* the murderer, then he'll go to prison and there won't be any money and Andrew will have to lose Greta after all, and that would be awful!"

"Ma, what on earth are you talking about?"

"Oh, it's too complicated to explain. Shall we stop and get something to eat on the way back to save cooking when we get home?"

I didn't feel I could ring Roger up and question him about Clive out of the blue, as it were, but fortunately I ran into him at a piano recital at Brunswick Lodge while we were both collecting our refreshments (a statutory glass of wine and a ham vol-au-vent) in the interval.

"Hello, Sheila, nice to see you. He's very good, isn't he? I thought he played the Schumann quite magnificently."

"Yes, he's marvelous. I heard him last year and I was determined not to miss this concert."

"Me, too. Jilly's not terribly keen, so she didn't come, although Rosemary offered to baby-sit."

"Look, Roger, I know this isn't really the time or the place, and it's mean to bother you when you're off-duty, but could I have a quick word—about Graham?"

Roger gave me a sharp look. "Yes, of course."

"Right," I said. "Well, let's just go into the small committee room where it's a bit quieter."

I led the way, out of the crush of people, along the corridor.

"Now then." Roger put his glass and plate on the table and sat down. "What's all this about?"

I sat down and took a sip of my wine for encouragement and said, "It's Clive Merivale, Graham's nephew. While I was at the funeral I discovered that he's pretty short of cash. Apparently they've been discussing fairly drastic entrenchment."

"I see."

"And, from the way he was going on, he seems very anxious to get his hands on Graham's money. There should be quite a bit, and as he and Angela were both at pains to tell me, they *were* his only relatives."

"Hmm." Roger made a noncommittal noise.

"And," I continued, "he was going round Graham's flat (I met him there to hand over Graham's things) more or less pricing everything and planning to sell the lease. . . ."

Roger took a cautious sip from his glass. "What do you think this wine is? They just said 'red or white?' so it could be anything!"

"So you do see," I persisted, "that he does seem to have a really strong motive. And, really, as far as I can see, nobody else has."

Roger put down his glass. "You're right, of course. He does seem to be the only person—as far as we know—to have a pretty powerful motive. Unfortunately he also has an alibi."

"You mean business in Leeds?" I asked. "But I really don't think he was there. I asked him about it— quite casually, you know—and he was really evasive. So he might not have been there at all."

"He wasn't."

"What!"

Roger gave what, in anyone I wasn't fond of, I would have called a smirk. "You underestimate me, my dear Watson," he said. "I did check, you know."

"And?"

"Well, I shouldn't be telling you this, but since you've already convicted the wretched man in your own mind, you'd better know the truth. I'm sure I can rely on your discretion."

"Yes, of course," I said impatiently. "Where was he, then?"

"Dewsbury."

"*Dewsbury!* What on earth was he doing there, and why didn't he say so in the first place?"

"*Cherchez la femme.*"

"What the . . . Oh, you mean he has a girlfriend!"

"That's right. A girl—much younger than him—called Vicky. She confirmed that he was with her until midday on the day of the murder. So he couldn't have done it."

"A girlfriend! Good heavens! Mind you, I can see that anyone with a wife like Angela might need a Vicky in their life." I paused to consider the implications. "But, surely, if that's the setup, Clive could have easily persuaded her to give him an alibi even if he wasn't there."

"Well, no, as it happens. There was an independent witness. Her mother."

"Her mother!"

"Vicky lives with her mother, who, as you might imagine, doesn't approve of these goings-on but can't do anything about it because it's Vicky who pays the rent."

"Oh."

"Highly vocal she was—long diatribe about the morals of the younger generation—and would have been very willing to do our friend Clive a bad turn if she could, but she had to admit that he'd been there when he said he had."

"Oh, well, in that case . . . How on earth did you get it out of him?" I asked curiously.

"It wasn't difficult. As you saw yourself, he was a bit evasive about his actual whereabouts, and it was obvious that I would check any story about a hotel in Leeds, and then his wife would get to know about it. So I did the 'utmost discretion' bit and the 'all chaps together' line and he was quite forthcoming."

"Oh, dear, and he did have such a good motive," I said regretfully. "I suppose it couldn't have been Angela?"

"The au pair—Greta, is that her name?—says Angela didn't leave for work until ten o'clock that morning." Roger gave me a quizzical look. "We did check that, too."

"I'm sorry, Roger," I said, feeling definitely foolish. "I didn't mean to imply . . ."

He smiled. "Don't mention it. You know I value your opinions. You carry on having them." He drained his glass. "I think I can hear people going back for the second half. Shall we go?" He looked at the rather shriveled vol-au-vent on his plate. "I don't think I can face this. Help me find somewhere on the way to dump it."

"I must say I did feel an absolute idiot," I said to Michael, when I got home. "It looked as if I hadn't trusted him to do his job!"

"Oh, Roger's a good sort, I don't suppose he took offense."

"No" I said ruefully, "more amused than anything."

I stirred a little hot water onto the drinking chocolate to mix it. "Will you have a cup?"

"Yes, please. And are there any of those cheesey biscuits left? I'm still a bit peckish." I handed him the tin and he took a handful. "So that's that, then? Blank wall, cul-de-sac, finis."

"Well, no, not exactly. There are a couple of other leads that I might follow up."

"But, Ma," Michael said, "need you go on? Why not leave it all to Roger? He's very competent—if anyone can solve it, he can."

"Yes, I know all that. But, well, Graham was an old friend (even if I didn't particularly like him), and he was staying here when it happened . . ."

"'What! in our house!'" Michael interjected. I ignored him and continued.

"I sort of feel I've got a responsibility to do what I can."

"The sacred laws of hospitality do not necessarily require you to track down his murderer."

"No, it's not that, it's just—oh, I don't know—just

a *feeling* I've got that I must go on while there's any sort of lead that I can do something about."

"If there are any other leads, why didn't you tell Roger?"

"I suppose I felt so foolish, having worked myself up about the Clive thing, only to be so thoroughly deflated!"

"So what are these leads, then?"

I took the cups of chocolate over to the kitchen table and sat down.

"I didn't tell you about the messages on Graham's answerphone, did I?" A thought struck me. "Goodness, I wonder if Roger's been to Graham's flat—I suppose he might have—and if he did I suppose he'd have played back the messages, too."

"Ma! You didn't!"

"Well," I said defensively, "it was a spur of the moment thing. Anyway, it's just as well I did because there were a couple of messages from Paul and one from Bryan, and all very peculiar." I took a comforting sip of chocolate. "Of course, if Roger *did* play those messages back, *he* had no means of knowing who they were from. I only did because I recognized the voices; they didn't identify themselves at all. I got the impression that they'd both been leaving messages like that over a period of time."

"What did they say?" Michael asked.

"Well, Paul left two messages, both a bit frantic, asking Graham to get in touch with him because 'things were getting out of hand,' whatever that might mean. I suppose it could be that business about the boundary dispute."

"From what you've told me," Michael said judicially, "it sounds as if that particular business had got right out of hand already! And what about Bryan?"

"That was *very* peculiar. Hang on, I wrote it down in my diary after I'd had lunch with Clive so that I wouldn't get it wrong." I rummaged in my handbag and found my diary. "Yes, here we are. 'I refer you to Section 36 of the Trustee Act 1925, and I'll see you in hell first.' What do you make of that?"

"Good God!" Michael reached up and took a large and imposing volume from one of the bookshelves and leafed through the pages. "Yes, here we are. 1925, did you say?" He read for a while and then continued, "Yes, well, it's all about Trust Instruments. If Bryan was concerned with a Trust and if Graham had drawn it up, under this Act, he would have had the power of appointing Trustees vested in himself. He could be the sole Trustee, so no one else could get at it and he could never be deposed. In other words, he could do what he jolly well liked."

"But surely Bryan would never have agreed to that!"

"It depends how good he was at understanding legal gobbledegook and how far he trusted his old mate Graham."

"And the message he left on the answerphone," I said, slowly working it out, "seems to indicate that he'd just found out and was absolutely furious about it."

"Could be."

"Would he be able to break the Trust? I mean, if he hadn't realized just what Graham had done?"

"That would depend on a lot of things, but it would be pretty difficult."

I got up and took the mugs over to the sink. "What I can't understand is why Graham did all these extraordinary things to people who are supposed to be his friends. I mean, is it just that he's a bad solicitor, not realizing what he's doing, or—and I find this very hard to believe—is it some Machiavellian plot to extort money?"

Michael frowned. "Well, we've always known that he's a rotten solicitor. If you remember, Father always said so, and we've often wondered how he came to be made a senior partner in that rather grand firm."

"So you think there's something more sinister, then?"

"I honestly don't know. He does have some fairly useful clients who've stuck with him through thick and thin over the years."

"But if he's so inefficient, as you say, *why* have they stayed with him?" I asked.

"Search me! Unless he knows some sort of guilty secret!"

"Well, that might apply to one of them, but hardly to them all! No, it's very strange." I rinsed the sediment of cocoa out of the mugs and put them in the dishwasher. "Anyway, I'm going to poke about and see what I can find."

"Do be careful, Ma, you never know *what* you may find!"

"I think I'll start with Paul," I said. "He did invite me over, so I'll ring up and say I'm going to be in that part of the county and can I drop in."

Michael sighed. "Oh, well, if you've got the bit between your teeth, nothing *I* can say will stop you. It'll probably all be a wild goose chase."

"Oh, dear, I do hope not," I said, laughing, "not geese as well. Alice's goats are going to be bad enough without that!"

· 9 ·

Hartland House is on the other side of the county from Taviscombe. It is an elegant Regency building standing in formal parkland, with immemorial oaks, an ancient cedar tree on the lawn, a small folly, and everything handsome about it. But as I drove up the drive I couldn't help noticing that it badly needed resurfacing, and as I stood on the curved stone steps, wrestling with the massive brass bell-pull, I saw that the plaster was coming away from the pillars on either side of the doorway.

Paul came to the door holding a drying-up cloth in his hand.

"Hello, Sheila, splendid to see you. You remembered the way here all right?"

"Well, I did get lost in that bit by Slattenslade—such a marvelous name!—and found myself in the middle of a farmyard, but that's par for the course for me!"

"Good, good, come on in. Alice is out in the dairy."

The entrance hall with its massive brass lantern was as impressive as ever, as was the exquisite sweep of the fine staircase, up three flights to the great glass dome above. But, as I followed Paul out through the kitchen quarters toward the dairy, I was aware of a degree of dilapidation, a lapse from former high standards—to be frank, the passages were not very clean, the stone flags unwashed (unswept even, in places), the walls and ceilings cobwebby.

In the dairy, a cold, rather dank room, whose small window, overhung by low eaves, let in the minimum of light, Alice was crouched over an enormous bowl doing something complicated with butter, muslin, and a large jug of what looked like sour milk. She looked up briefly as Paul and I came in.

"Oh, Sheila—I'll be with you in a minute when I've strained these curds."

"Oh"—I assumed an interested expression—"are you making cheese? How splendid."

"The goats," Paul said with a degree of asperity in his voice, "produce an inordinate quantity of milk that no one seems to want. We have tried to sell it, but it's a very complicated business—all sorts of rules and regulations. So Alice has taken to turning it into cheese."

"Goat's milk is supposed to be very good for you, isn't it? And, of course, there are some people who can't drink cow's milk. . . ."

"Well," Paul said, "they don't seem to live round here. We couldn't *give* the stuff away!"

"Well," I said brightly, "I'm sure the cheese is delicious. Very fashionable now—all those delicious recipes for Greek feta cheese." Alice put the jug down and squeezed the excess liquid from the muslin. "There," she said, "that'll do for now." She wiped her hands on an old tea towel. "We'll go and have tea."

Tea had been set out in the library, a handsome room, book-lined and hung with large, ornately framed pictures, the subjects of which were barely discernible through the ancient, discolored varnish. Most of the books were old and, I assume, valuable; at least they were bound in leather, with faded gilt lettering on the spine. Paul's own books, those that he had written, were housed elsewhere.

Tea was already laid out on the massive round table by the window. There was a plate of roughly cut sandwiches, some home-made biscuits, in whose manufacture oatmeal seemed to have played a major part, and a heavy-looking fruitcake.

"How do you like your tea?" Alice asked.

"Oh, weak and without milk," I said hastily as she raised a jug undoubtedly containing goat's milk. "Thank you, that's fine."

I put my cup on a small brass table and went to sit down. My foot caught in the frayed edge of the rug and I almost fell.

"Oh, dear, are you all right, Sheila?" Paul asked anxiously. "We keep meaning to have that rug mended—it's one my father brought back from Persia in the 1930s. . . ."

I sat down in one of the chintz-covered armchairs, whose armpieces were almost as frayed as the rug. Alice must have seen me looking at it because she said, "I really must do something about these covers, they're practically falling to pieces! But you know how difficult it is to find just the right material. . . ."

"Oh, yes," I said, "and it would mean a trip to Bath or London to find anything really suitable."

"And, really," Alice continued, "I don't know *when* I would find the time."

"No," I agreed. "I'm sure it must be a full-time job to look after the goats and the bees and things."

There was a silence, during which I managed to swallow the last soggy remnants of my tomato sandwich and sip a little of my tea, which was Earl Grey and mercifully quite drinkable.

Alice offered me a slice of cake and seemed quite relieved when I refused. Looking at it in its solid, uncut state, I wondered if it was simply a cake for show, to be offered but never consumed.

"Well," Paul said, "it's lovely to see you here, Sheila. It's been ages!"

"Since I've been to Hartland? Yes, indeed. Though of course I saw you quite recently at Graham's funeral."

At the mention of Graham's name I was aware of a sort of tension between Paul and Alice.

"Yes, of course," Paul said. "Very sad. Not many there. Still, I'm glad I was able to make it."

"Yes, me too."

"Did you gather anything about the will? Does the nephew get everything? He spent a lot of time talking to that lawyer person at the funeral."

"I don't know. I imagine so; there isn't really anyone else, is there?"

"They seem to be pretty well off, didn't you think? The whole house smelt of money!"

"Well, yes, I'd think their lifestyle was pretty extravagant."

I saw no need to tell Paul about Andrew's revelation.

"Needs a bit of keeping up."

"Yes, I suppose so."

There was a pause and then Paul asked, "Any more news from the police?"

I shook my head. "Not really. Well, there was one thing." After all Paul's heavy-handed hints about Clive, I couldn't resist saying, "They've definitely cleared Clive."

"What!" Paul gave me a very sharp look.

"Chief Inspector Eliot told me that he had a cast-iron alibi."

"Oh, I see. That's that, then."

"Stronger than the rest of us," I continued. "Well me, certainly. I was just at home, mostly by myself. Though Michael was at work, and you—you were in London, weren't you?"

"Yes, I had to see my publisher. We had lunch at that new place in Covent Garden. Very good."

"Lovely. It really is a bit of a bore getting up to London now. There are hardly any trains. If you want to be sure of being there by lunchtime you have to get that nine o'clock one, which is always dreadfully crowded. I usually get the very early one, the 6:45, which means getting up at crack of dawn, but it's worth it."

"Yes," Paul said, "that's the one I got. The trains are impossible now, but it's even worse to go by car—absolutely nowhere to park."

"Still, I did manage quite well when I went up for the funeral. I was very lucky with taxis, which was just as well, with Graham's suitcase and everything. I did tell you, didn't I, that I met Clive at Graham's flat? Goodness, it's a gloomy place. Have you ever been there? Full of the most incredibly old-fashioned furniture. Like a time warp! I'm sure that if you switched on the television set you'd get pictures of the Coronation! In fact, the only modern thing he had was an answerphone. Still, I suppose he had to have that for his work, don't you think?"

As I mentioned the answerphone I looked directly at Paul and saw a question in his eyes. Was he wondering if I had somehow heard his message? And, if so, what had I made of it? Or of the papers he must have known Graham had with him when he was killed?

"I—we," Paul said, "used to go there occasionally, but not for ages. As you say, it was a gloomy sort of place." He finished the remains of his tea and got up. "Now you really must come and see the goats, mustn't she, Alice?"

Alice, who had been uncharacteristically silent during this exchange, also got up and led the way out, through the stone flagged passages at the back, into the yard outside, and thence into one of the paddocks where four goats were tethered. They stopped cropping the grass as we approached and raised their heads, fixing us with their bold, yellow eyes. I have always been nervous of goats, ever since one of the wild ones at Lynton roughly snatched my ice cream cone when I was a child, so I didn't venture too near, merely expressing admiration from a distance. Mercifully this seemed to be enough, and Alice then announced that we would visit the beehives in the orchard. Since I am even more frightened of bees than I am of goats, this wasn't a great improvement. Still, I managed to insert a few disconnected words of praise into Alice's monologue about the glories of beekeeping and followed with relief when Alice took us all off to see the improvements they had made to the henhouse.

As we walked through the grounds I wondered idly which was the boundary that all the trouble was about, but I couldn't think of any way of introducing the subject.

The gardens, which Alice had designed some years ago, were still lovely, although I noticed that there was a certain amount of unpruned growth and more weeds than she would normally have allowed.

"Have you still got that marvelous gardener?" I asked. "Mortimer? Was that his name?"

"Oh, we had to let him go," Paul said. "He was getting very old. We manage quite well ourselves now. . . ."

Alice shot him an angry look but didn't say anything.

"It all looks very lovely," I said soothingly. "You laid it out so beautifully, Alice. Have you had many commissions lately?"

"Not many, people don't seem to have the money. . . . Besides," she went on, a resentful note coming into her voice, "I simply haven't the time to do anything nowadays, I always seem to be busy in the house."

I couldn't actually see any difference to the henhouse, but I assumed an expression of polite interest as Paul explained several structural alterations he had made. It seemed that as well as housework and gardening, he was now having to do odd jobs of carpentry.

"Goodness," I said, "how clever of you to do it all yourself. When do you find the time?"

"Oh," Paul said airily, "I find a certain amount of manual labor is very refreshing after sitting in libraries or at my word processor for hours on end."

"Yes, I suppose so. And being out in the fresh air must do you good. I know Graham always used to say that walking to work every morning across the park always set him up for the day."

"Yes," Paul said, "poor old Graham." A sound like an indignant snort came from Alice, but Paul ignored her and went on, "It's always sad when one of the circle goes, someone you've known all your life. And then, of course, Alec is in a pretty bad way now. I went to see him at the beginning of the year, and it was really depressing to see him stuck in that wheelchair. Oh, he seemed to be his old self—you know, the usual sardonic humor—but it seemed to me that he was getting very bitter."

"Yes, that was a tragedy. I suppose it's progressive—it'll never get any better?"

"No. He's fairly helpless, I think. Fortunately he's got Penrose, quite a character, otherwise I don't know what he'd do."

"Still," I said, "Alec Patmore's case is quite different. Graham was murdered, after all."

They both reacted differently to the word. Paul look away, as if embarrassed, but there was a look almost of triumph on Alice's face.

"Yes, quite extraordinary," Paul said hastily. "I mean, it isn't something that happens to people one actually *knows*, is it?"

"What I can't understand," I said, "is who on earth would have a motive for actually killing someone as harmless as Graham?"

"Harmless!" Alice exclaimed. "Harmless? Graham Percy!" Paul tried to interrupt, but she went on, "He was a destructive, evil man! He brought nothing but trouble and ruin. I hated him and I'm glad that he's dead!"

Her eyes were blazing and her face was twisted with emotion. I wondered, for a moment, if Alice might not have passed the borders of eccentricity to some other, more sinister territory. After a moment she turned abruptly and went off toward the far part of the garden.

There was an awkward silence, then Paul said lamely, "I'm sorry, Alice has been under a bit of a strain lately, what with one thing and another. . . ."

"Yes, of course," I said. "We're all doing more than we ought to, don't you find? And it does take it out of one. Goodness, is that the time? I really must be getting on. It's been lovely seeing you both. Do say good-bye to Alice for me—I really must dash."

Driving home, I thought about Alice's outburst. Perhaps it was just a general feeling of fury at Graham's incompetence, which had led to their obvious financial difficulties, but I wondered if there might not be something more behind it. Alice was an intense sort of person, capable of goodness knows what, and, while it seemed that Paul had an alibi, nothing had been said about Alice's movements on the morning Graham was murdered.

· 10 ·

"But, Ma," Michael said, when I propounded this theory, "can you see Alice Heywood murdering Graham?"

"Well, yes," I replied, "as a matter of fact I can. I know she's normally frightfully vague and wispy, but you didn't see her today—all twisted with fury. I suppose it's because of that wretched boundary thing and the money it's cost them. I must say, everything did look dreadfully run-down there."

"Well, at least now that Graham's out of the way they may not go to the Court of Appeal—at least not if, as you seem to think, they didn't want to get in this deep in the first place."

"Those calls that Paul left on Graham's answerphone didn't sound like those of an enthusiastic plaintiff."

"In that case they can simply instruct whoever takes over Graham's cases to go for an out-of-court settlement."

"But they've still spent an awful lot of money! Do you think they might be able to sue the firm for unsuitable advice or whatever you call it?"

"It's possible. Lawyers have oodles of insurance for just such contingencies. But I still can't understand how Graham, who's supposed to be such a chum, could have got them into this ghastly situation in the first place!"

"I suppose he might have some sort of hold over them."

"You suggested that before," Michael said reflectively, "and for Bryan Shelley and that Trust thing. But can you think of Graham—boring old Graham—as a sinister blackmailer?"

"Well, now you put it like that . . . I wonder!"

"What?"

"It's just occurred to me. Paul said he got the early train to London from Taunton—the six something, I can't remember the time exactly—so he would have left the house at crack of dawn. *But* he could still have managed to get up to London by lunchtime if he'd caught the nine o'clock train. So. He could have driven over to Taviscombe, murdered Graham sometime between half past seven and eight (he could have got here easily by then), and then driven on to Taunton and got the nine o'clock train!"

"And the motive?"

"Money, of course. What had already gone and the possibility of a new and, it seems likely, continuing drain on their resources."

"Mm." Michael seemed doubtful.

"It does seem to have hit them hard," I said, "this money thing. Alice was really very upset, and although Paul appeared quite chatty, he was definitely edgy, not really his old self. I don't know how much money they have. Paul can't make that much from his books—I mean, they're splendid and tremendously well received by the critics, but not what you'd call popular successes—or Alice from her gardens. I believe Paul inherited a bit, but a place like Hartland House is terribly expensive to keep up nowadays. Quite possibly, if things had gone on with Graham, then they might have had to sell up, and that would have broken their hearts. Oh, I think there was a motive there, all right."

"You're probably right."

"I wonder about that train!" I said. "But there's no way to prove it. I can't very well go and question the booking clerk at the station. I wonder if Roger has? And then there's Alice—has *she* got an alibi? Oh, it's *so* frustrating!"

"Why don't you ring Roger up and ask?"

"No, I can't now, not after that business of Clive Merivale, I'd be too embarrassed. Oh, well, I'll just have to hope I bump into him somewhere and then try and introduce the subject casually into the conversation."

Michael laughed. "That I would like to hear!"

As it turned out I didn't have to. I was chatting to Rosemary the following day when she asked, "How did your visit to the Heywoods go? Is Alice as dotty as ever?"

"More or less," I said. "Still very goat- and bee-oriented. But it's sad, really, the house is looking desperately run-down and even the garden isn't what it was."

"Really?" She poured herself another cup of coffee. "You'll have a top-up, won't you? Actually I haven't been over for ages. What do you think's happened there?"

"Money problems, I think."

"Oh, that would explain it."

I looked at her enquiringly.

"Jack traveled up to London with Paul a little while ago, and he said he seemed a bit peculiar."

"Peculiar?"

"Edgy is what Jack said, as if his mind was elsewhere. You know how he's usually such a *positive* sort of person."

"You don't happen to remember when this was? When Jack went to London?"

"As a matter of fact I do. It was the day your chum Graham was killed."

"Ah."

Rosemary looked at me sideways.

"Are you doing your sleuthing bit again?" she asked.

"Sort of. Which train did Jack get? Was it the five past nine?"

"No, it was that ghastly early one—quarter to

seven, I think it is—because he had to be in Holborn
by nine-thirty."

"Bother."

"That isn't what you wanted to hear?"

"Not really."

"Oh, well, have a biscuit and leave all that sort of
thing to Roger."

"I have, really. It's just that I find myself wondering . . ."

"Anyway, I'd think Alice is a far more likely murder suspect than Paul."

"Do you? Why?"

"More irrational, more unbalanced. But what on
earth would be the motive for either of them to kill
Graham? I thought he was a friend of theirs?"

I didn't feel I could tell Rosemary about looking
at Graham's papers or listening to his answerphone,
so I said vaguely, "Oh, no motive that I know of—I
was just considering everyone who knew him, people he stayed with, that is."

"Even Alec Patmore?"

"Well, no, hardly, since he's been in a wheelchair
for years now."

"Pity. He'd make a marvelous villain. Do you remember his Iago? Really *evil*. Or his Cardinal in *The
Duchess of Malfi*? Tremendously sinister!"

"Yes, wasn't he marvelous! Oh, well, life is never
as simple as that—just *looking* like a villain isn't
enough."

"So that's Paul in the clear," I reported back to
Michael. "And it will probably turn out that Alice

was with the local bee-keeper or the vet, and the goats were farrowing or kidding, or whatever they do. I can't see any way of finding out. I must just keep my ears open and leave it to fortune."

Fortune did, however, appear to be on my side for once, since a few days later I had a phone call from my friend David Beaumont. David is an actor—well, was, really, since now he runs the Shakespeare Institute in Stratford-on-Avon.

"Sheila, darling, can I beg a bed for a couple of nights? Only I've got to go to Bath and I thought I'd kill two birds with one stone and see you and Michael on the way."

"Of course," I said. David is always a welcome guest. "How lovely! What are you going to Bath for?"

"Well, actually, I want to borrow some things for an exhibition I'm mounting at the Institute. Alec Patmore has some very interesting Irving things and some wonderful set designs for some of the Beerbohm Tree productions at His Majesty's."

"Alec Patmore!"

"Yes. Do you know him?"

"No, but I'd very much like to. David, you're an answer to my prayers!"

"More things are wrought by prayer than this world dreams of," David intoned in his Poetry Voice. "What *do* you mean?"

"I'll tell you when you come."

————

"So you see," I said, when David arrived and had been filled in on the details of the murder, "it really would be sort of helpful to see Alec Patmore. He might have something to say about Graham that might shed a little light on things."

"The most extraordinary thing to me," David said, "is the fact that Alec should have had a friend like this Graham person. I mean, from what you've told me, they couldn't have had a single thing in common. Certainly not enough for Alec to have him to *stay*! Especially now when he's so ill."

"They were at school together," I said, "and Oxford."

"Yes, but even so! Alec's never struck me as the sentimental type who liked to wallow in nostalgia about high jinks in the dorm and how we put a toad in Matron's bath. He certainly wasn't one to suffer fools gladly, and I gather that Graham Thing was *infinitely* tedious—well, you've said as much yourself."

"Frequently. He was. But you know how people can be about old ties."

"Yes, I suppose . . ." David said doubtfully.

"So could you, *please*, take me with you when you go and see him? You could say you're staying with us, and I've always been an admirer. Lay the admiration on a bit thick, if you like. Or wouldn't that go down well?"

"Alec is a sardonic so-and-so, but he's also an actor, and admiration to an actor can never be too fulsome."

"So you will?"

"Oh, all right, then, I'll ring and ask if I may bring you. Anyway, who am I to deny you a glimpse of your girlhood hero?"

"Actually I did stick a picture postcard of him as Berowne in the front of my Arden copy of *Love's Labor's Lost*. You know, that production at the Old Vic when he was quite young."

"God, yes, with Julia as Rosaline. Goodness, she was beautiful in those days! Pure Pre-Raphaelite, wonderful long neck, and she used to hold her head, just so—like Ellen, you know."

While David went on to recall old theatrical memories, I wondered just what else I might be able to find out about Graham.

Since Alec Patmore appeared to have no objection to my presence, David and I set off early the next day, had lunch on the way down, and arrived at the handsome house in Laura Place at about three o'clock.

The dresser, Penrose, opened the door. He was a tall, thin man, of indeterminate age, with hair whose blackness and glossiness looked as if it owed more to artifice than to nature. He was dressed in a black polo sweater and black jeans, though the generally somber effect was alleviated by a number of gold chains round his neck and his wrists.

"Oh, Mr. Beaumont and Mrs. Malory—is that right?—do come on in. *He's* having his rest, but I'll wake him in about half an hour. Would you like to go into the drawing room, or would you like to come and have a chat with me in the kitchen while you're waiting?"

We elected to follow him into the kitchen, which was a large airy room, with blue and white flowered curtains, a Welsh dresser laden with brightly colored crockery, an Aga, a heavy kitchen table covered with a deep blue chenille cloth, and several comfortable chairs. On the seat of one of the chairs, curled up on a patchwork cushion, was a large tabby cat. The whole thing looked exactly like the stage set of a kitchen in some 1930s comedy by Eden Philpotts. I caught David's eye and saw that he had the same reaction.

"Make yourselves comfy," Penrose said. "I won't be a sec, I just want to pop these scones in the oven." He turned and saw me stroking the cat. "Turf Trinculo off that chair—he always chooses the best one!" I picked up the cat, sat down, and settled it on my lap, stroking its large, handsome head.

"Trinculo?" I asked.

"Yes, we had two, but Stephano died last year—ever so cut up about it, he was."

Penrose opened the door of the Aga and slid a tray full of scones inside.

"How is Alec?" David asked.

"Up and down, dear, up and down. Some days he's quite his old self, quite bright, but others—well! Gloom, and moody with it. Still, it's not to be wondered at, I suppose, stuck in that thing."

"Does he ever go out?" I asked.

"Sometimes. On his good days I pop him in the

car and we go for a little run round. But he won't go
into the town anymore. I told him, no one's going to
look at *you*—but he won't be seen by His Public in
that wheelchair. Pride, I suppose. Silly, I call it."

"Still," I said, "you can understand how he feels."

"Well, yes, in a way you're right, dear. But I say,
why deny yourself the few pleasures left to you out
of pride. Not," he said, spreading a sheet of newspaper over the table, "that I fancy pushing a wheelchair up and down these ghastly hills. Honestly, it
takes years off you traipsing up and down with the
shopping—I mean, you can't find *anywhere* to park
now, so you can't take the car, and most of the
things *he* likes you can't get in supermarkets that
have proper car parks."

He picked up a collection of shoes from the floor
and started to polish them. "You don't mind me getting on with these, do you? But what with one thing
and another I'm all behind today." He spread polish
carefully onto a brown shoe and began to rub at it
with a soft cloth.

"That's a handsome pair of brogues," David said.

"Handmade by Lobbs in London," Penrose said,
breathing lightly on the leather and rubbing away at
it with a circular movement. "Lovely, aren't they?
Always had his shoes made there—a pair every
year, even now. These are the latest pair. They make
them on his own last there, of course. And Mr. Maurice, too—comes down every year from Staggs in
Savile Row to fit his new suit. He won't give in, you

see." He looked at us defiantly, as if challenging us to contradict him.

"I think that's marvelous," I said softly.

He gave me a grateful glance and went on polishing.

"I hope he wasn't too upset about Mr. Percy's death," I said.

"Mr. Percy?" He looked at me sharply. "Oh, of *course*, you're *that* Mrs. Malory, the lady who phoned me! Silly me! The name didn't ring a bell—though I did think the voice was familiar when you spoke just now! Well! What a coincidence that you should be a friend of Mr. Beaumont here!"

"Yes, isn't it!"

"Yes, well, he was *quite* upset when I told him. Such a nasty business, murder. Still, you know how it is, you try and put these things out of your mind, don't you? And *I* wasn't going to let him dwell on it. He's got quite enough to depress him these days!"

"Yes, of course."

There was a brief silence in which the only sounds were the ticking of the large wall-clock and Trinculo's loud purr.

"It must be a lot of work for you, having people stay," I said.

Penrose put the polished shoes down on the floor, folded the newspaper, and put it in a pedal bin.

"Oh, it's nothing to what it used to be in the old days. A *houseful* we had then. Everyone came— Larry and Viv, Cecil, Noël and Graham, John G.,

Ralph, oh, *everyone*—especially when Madam and he were together." He sighed. "Those were the days, all right."

"You must miss it all," David said, "and I suppose Alec does, too."

Penrose shrugged. "It wasn't the same when Madam went. He didn't see many people then. It was just work, work, work—really threw himself into it, as you might say. And then, when he got ill . . ."

"But he still saw people?"

"Just a few old friends, not people in the profession—well, perhaps one or two, but not parties or anything like that."

"My friend Paul Heywood said he saw him a little while ago," I said. "I think he was very sad to see how ill Sir Alec had become."

"Oh, Mr. Heywood—*such* a nice person, very appreciative. He's one who really does enjoy his food, he's a pleasure to cook for. Do you know, he ate a whole *plate* of brownies I made last time he was here! Oh, yes, a very nice gentleman."

"And Mr. Percy," I asked, "did you like him?"

Penrose gave me a straight look. "Well, no, dear, now you come to ask, I wasn't very struck."

"Really?"

"A *difficult* gentleman, picky, if you know what I mean."

"Oh, yes, I know," I said. "He could be maddening. He was a friend of my late husband, actually,"

I went on, hoping to elicit further confidences, "not mine."

"Well, then, you'll know what I mean. Nothing ever right for him."

"Oh, I know!"

Encouraged by my tone, Penrose leaned forward confidentially. "Quite honestly, I used to be surprised at the way *he* put up with it, especially since he's never been one to suffer fools gladly. But there, they've known each other forever, and Mr. Percy always took it for granted, as you might say, that he'd be welcome. A hide like a rhinoceros, too! You could cut the atmosphere with a knife sometimes at dinner, when I took the food in. I hardly knew where to look! But then I've always been *very* sensitive to atmosphere."

"Did they quarrel?" David asked curiously.

"Oh, no, nothing like that. I shouldn't think it would be easy to pick a quarrel with Mr. Percy. I don't expect he'd notice if you did! No, *he'd* make one of his sarcastic remarks, and Mr. Percy'd pretend he didn't know what he meant. But he did all right."

"Don't I know it!" David laughed. "You always know when Alec's given you a set-down! 'I'd put her in her place, if she *had* a place.' Do you remember?"

"A wicked tongue he's got," Penrose said with pride, "always had. Made a lot of enemies in the old days."

"God, yes, I remember that production of the

Dream, when he was playing Oberon. Richard Boreman very nearly walked out, you know—well, he really wasn't up to playing Theseus, and he knew it. Poor Tyrone had a hell of a time persuading him not to!"

"You were playing Lysander, weren't you?" Penrose said. "I remember now. That purple velvet number you had in the last act, with fur trimming at the neck—really lovely, suited you a treat. I bet you couldn't get into it now!"

David looked at his waistline regretfully. "I don't suppose I could. 'Old, old Master Shallow. We have seen the best of our time. . . .' "

His voice faded away and there was a moment's silence. Then Penrose said, "Look at the time! He'll be stirring any minute now."

He snatched a cloth and took the tray of scones, now a delicious golden brown, out of the Aga. "I'll just pop these into the warming oven and put the kettle on. There we are. Now, come with me—I'll just wheel the trolley into the drawing room and go and see to him."

"How does he manage the stairs?" David asked.

"Oh, we had a lift put in. *That* cost a pretty penny, I can tell you. But he couldn't manage without. He'd never have his bed brought down—that would be giving in and he'll never do that!"

He opened the door of the drawing room and we went in.

"Make yourselves at home, I won't be a sec."

He whisked out of the room, shutting the door behind him.

"Are all dressers like that?" I asked David.

"Alas, no. Penrose is one of the old school. He's been with Alec for years, ever since that first season at the Old Vic, and he's utterly devoted, he'd do anything in the world for him. Just as well, really, the way things have turned out. I don't suppose you could *buy* that devotion."

"Anything in the world . . ." I echoed. "No, there are some things you can't buy."

I looked round the drawing room—well, it was half drawing room (elegant Regency furniture and hangings) and half museum (objects in glass cases, framed playbills, and portraits of actors in heavy gilt frames). I moved across to look at one of the glass cases.

"Goodness," I said, "everything's labeled, just like a museum!" I bent forward to examine the exhibits. It was not easy to read the labels since the room was rather dark, the heavy brocade curtains being drawn back in great loops.

" 'Gloves worn by Ellen Terry in *The Merchant of Venice*; ring worn by Irving in *The Lyons Mail*; dagger used by Macready in *Macbeth*; and'—goodness, these are really terrific—'ivory comb belonging to Mrs. Siddons; and shoe buckles worn by David Garrick in *The Recruiting Officer*.' "

"Alec's been amassing things for years," David said. "The collection's quite famous. He's got some really fabulous things, costumes and so forth, stored away. I suppose he'll eventually leave them to the Theatre Museum or somewhere like that. It would be a crime if the collection was broken up."

"Actually, David, dear boy"—a voice in the doorway made us turn round—"I had thought of giving all the Shakespearean stuff to your Institute."

Alec Patmore was always a man of stature, in every respect, and even in a wheelchair he was a striking figure. As Penrose had told us he would be, he was impeccably dressed in an elegant gray suit with a double-breasted waistcoat, the shirt was obviously made in Jermyn Street, and the tie, I was prepared to bet, was a silk one from Sulka. The famous saturnine features were the same, as was the beautiful voice, but the once noble form was shrunk and bowed, the hands, expertly guiding the wheelchair, seemed gnarled and twisted, the legs covered by a rug. He had become an old man.

"Alec!" David moved quickly forward. "Marvelous to see you. You're looking splendid!"

"Liar! I look like the wreck that I am."

David laughed. "Have it your own way. But, Alec, did you really mean that? About leaving part of your collection to the Institute?"

"I said giving, not leaving. You might as well have it now—I'm not going to be able to enjoy it much longer."

"For heaven's sake! You've got years ahead of you!"

"Possibly, but I have decided it is time I settled

my affairs, and since on the whole I approve of what you're doing at Stratford, and since I know you care about the theater—even if you did sell out for a time to that deplorable incubus, television—you seem to me to be a suitable person to have charge of them." He spun his wheelchair round with a dramatic gesture. "What do you think, Mrs. Malory?"

Taken aback at this sudden attention, I stammered, "I can't think of anyone more suitable than David."

"Absolutely right. Do, please, sit down. I think I hear Penrose with the tea. As the only lady present, will you do us the honor of pouring for us?"

Penrose put two silver teapots and a hot water jug in front of me. "That one's Earl Grey and that's Indian—*he* likes Indian, but you looked like an Earl Grey person to me. The scones are under that cover, there. Eat them up while they're nice and warm."

"Thank you, Penrose," Alec Patmore said firmly, "that will be all."

Penrose moved obediently to the door, saying over his shoulder, "Just ring if you want any more hot water."

As I poured the tea and David passed round the scones, our host said amiably, "This is very nice. It was good of you, David, to bring me such a charming visitor."

"It was very kind of you to allow me to come," I said. "I've admired your work for so long."

Like most people, I suppose, when confronted by the object of my admiration, I'm always a little tongue-tied; but for all his formidable reputation, Alec Patmore was surprisingly easy to talk to. His passion for the theater was obvious, and he was only too willing to talk about the great productions he had been in and seemed pleased when I recalled various moments that I remembered with especial pleasure.

"Your Iago! That moment when you simply stood there, all alone center stage, silently shaking with laughter—goodness, it was chilling!"

"Iago is a gift, of course. It's all there in the words, the rhythms. Great evil is very simple. It's the half-shades, the noble mind corrupted, like Macbeth, for instance, that are almost impossible. More worth-while to attempt, perhaps, since they reflect life so much more precisely. With total evil one must bring out the comedy—the black humor—Richard the Third, Iago, too."

"Oh, yes, and Volpone," I said. "Volpone is almost my favorite of your roles! Literally *bouncing* up and down on that great bed with delight at gulling the poor fools you had deceived!"

"Ah, yes, Volpone. The Fox!" He leaned back in his wheelchair and crossed his hands in front of his chest, and, even without the russet beard and the makeup, his face became a vulpine mask. " 'Suns that set may rise again; but if once we lose this light, 'tis with us perpetual night.' " His voice broke. "Perpetual night," he repeated softly. I felt the tears coming to my eyes and lowered my head to brush them away.

"You can still do it, damn you," David said. "You can still do it."

Alex Patmore laughed. "A trick, technique—you should know that, David."

"But a gift, too," I protested, "the gift of being able to become someone else. And the perception, surely, to evaluate a character—how he speaks, how he moves, how he thinks."

"Trying to find the key to a character can be the devil and all," David said reflectively. "Bad enough in a modern play when you've got the author on hand to help if you get into deep water, but in Shakespeare, for example, you're on your own. That's why there are so many interpretations of the great roles. Everyone sees a different person."

"In life, too, I believe." Alec Patmore nodded. "So tell me, Mrs. Malory—or, since you are an old friend of my old friend here, I will call you Sheila and you shall call me Alec—tell me, Sheila, what did you think of Graham Percy?"

I was taken aback by the sudden question and stared at him without replying.

He smiled. "Penrose informs me that you were the friend with whom Graham was staying when he met his untimely end."

I tried to recover myself and said, "Yes, yes, I was." I paused for a moment, then I went on, "What did I think of Graham? I don't know, really. He's been a fixture in our lives for so long! He was a friend of my husband, well, not even a friend, really. They met when they were both young men, at the

College of Law. And Graham sort of *attached* himself and he's been around ever since."

"Did you like him?"

"Like him?" I echoed. "Well, no, actually, I don't think I did. I was *sorry* for him in a way and he was always so sure that we'd be glad to see him. But, if one gets down to it, he wasn't exactly a likable person." I was aware of his sharp gaze upon me, and on an impulse I asked, "And you? Did you like him?"

Alec Patmore gave me his slow, foxy smile, the smile I had admired so much in performance. "No," he said briskly. "Not at all."

"Then why . . . ?"

"Why did I put up with him all these years? My dear Sheila, why did you? No, Graham Percy was the sort of man whom nobody likes but to whom nobody can quite bring themselves to deal the coup de grâce."

"Except," David said, "that somebody did. And in a very final way."

"True, very true. Perhaps that was the only way to convince him that he wasn't liked. . . ." He turned to me. "Do the police have any idea who might have killed him? Are there any *clues*? Has a motive been revealed?"

"No," I said, "nothing. The police don't seem to be making any sort of progress."

"And you?" Alec Patmore enquired. "Do you have any theories?"

"Not really. I did wonder about his nephew—he

inherits everything, you know—but he has a cast-iron alibi. And, apart from the money, there doesn't seem to be any other motive. Unless," I said, looking sideways at him, "there's something in his past we don't know about."

He gave me a bland smile. "That may well be. Apparently two-dimensional characters—and we are all agreed, are we not, that Graham was just such a one—quite often have dark secrets hidden deep in their past."

"But," I said, obscurely aware that I was participating in some sort of game of his devising, "you've known him since you were at school. Surely you would have known if there was such a secret?"

I caught the glint of approval in his eye and wondered what path he was leading me down.

"He was a very boring boy. As he was a very boring man."

Not a path, a cul-de-sac.

"So you know of no reason why anyone should have wanted to kill him?"

"The heart has its reasons. . . ."

"The heart? But I never knew that he had any kind of love affair!"

"He didn't. But others may have done, don't you think?"

"You think he may have known something about someone else's love affair . . ."

"Love takes many forms—for a person, for money, for some object, a house, maybe. Who knows?"

"But," I said, determined to pin him down, "you think Graham was killed because he knew something that someone else wanted kept a secret?"

"It would seem to be a *possibility*, don't you think?"

"Yes." I had the impression now that I was being led in circles. One thing was certain. Alec Patmore knew more about the reason for Graham's death than he was prepared to admit.

The door opened and Penrose came in.

"I'll just take these things out," he said, gathering up the cups and plates and wheeling the trolley toward the door. "Then I'll get the boxes with all the bits and bobs for Mr. Beaumont." He gave his master a critical look. "*You're* looking tired."

It was true. Alec Patmore did look exhausted; his dark eyes looked sunken in his white face, his shoulders more bowed than before.

David got to his feet.

"Goodness, yes. I'm so sorry, Alec. We've worn you out. Perhaps I could just have a quick word about the exhibition, then we'll be on our way."

I got up, too, and while they talked, wandered about the room, looking at the relics of the theatrical past and wondering why such ordinary things—a comb, a quizzing glass, a walking stick—should have become imbued with such significance, objects of interest, of reverence even, simply because they had been used, had been actually handled, by men and women whose names had lived on through the years even in such an ephemeral world as the the-

ater—as Alec Patmore's name would live on. Actors
are, indeed, the abstracts and brief chronicles of the
time and hold a mirror up to nature, showing us
ourselves and other people.

Alec had been trying to tell me something, I felt
sure, something he couldn't, or wouldn't, speak of
openly. I just wished I knew what it was. Alec Patmore, Bryan Shelley, and Paul Heywood had all
known Graham Percy for many years. He was, in
his legal capacity, involved in the lives of two of
them and a regular visitor in the home of all three.
Somewhere, buried deep in the past of this little
group, I was sure, was the motive for his death. But
how was I to find out what it was? Alec Patmore
was only prepared to give me tantalizing half-hints;
I would have to see what I could elicit from the
other two. Or Josh Brendon. He had known Graham, too. I suddenly remembered his words: "It's
about Graham. Something I found out—I think you
should know." Surely by now he would be back
from America. I decided I must ring him very soon.

"Right, then, Sheila." David's voice broke
through my thoughts. "I'll just go and collect those
boxes and we'll be off."

He went out in search of Penrose, and Alec Patmore wheeled himself over to the window where I
was standing.

"Thank you so much for a delightful afternoon,"
I said formally.

He smiled. "Thank you for coming. I hope you
will come again. I feel we have much to talk about.

Also you seem to have made a great hit with Penrose, so you see you will be especially welcome. Any time, I am always here." Again the smile.

"Thank you, I'd like that. And please tell Penrose that I'd love to have the recipe for those delicious scones."

Penrose came back into the room. "Mr. Beaumont's brought the car round, and he says could you go now because he can't park outside for more than a minute."

"Of course." I turned to Alec Penrose and held out my hand. "Good-bye and thank you." His hand was very cold and dry, like parchment.

"Good-bye," he said. "I will look forward to our next meeting."

As I got into the car I glanced back and saw them both framed in the doorway, as though on a stage set, Alec Patmore with his hand raised in a regal gesture of farewell, while Penrose, his hands grasping the back of the wheelchair, leaned forward protectively toward his master.

"Goodness," I said to David, "that *was* an experience!"

"Alec's always good value. Desperately sad to see him like that. Still, he seemed quite chirpy—a bit gnomic, I thought, at times, but definitely chirpy. He seemed to take to you."

"I was very nervous about meeting him, but he couldn't have been more charming."

"He always could turn on the charm when he wanted something."

But what, I wondered, could Alec Patmore want of me? To question the reasons for Graham's death, perhaps. But why?

We were driving through the center of Bath now, and my attention was diverted by a familiar sign in an unexpected place.

"Oh, do look, David! There's a McDonald's here now. All done up in the local stone, but definitely a hamburger joint, here in Bath. What *would* Jane Austen have said? Or her characters? Think how sarcastic Mr. Knightley would have been, or Mr. Darcy!"

"Oh, but think," David replied, "how Lydia and Kitty Bennet would have loved it! Hanging out at McDonald's would have been so much more fun than trailing into Merryton to catch a glimpse of the militia!"

· 12 ·

After David had gone back to Stratford I did try to ring Chillington, but evidently Josh wasn't back because I only got the answerphone, so all I could do was speculate about what he'd been going to tell me about Graham. Actually, I didn't have much time to do even that because I was suddenly caught up in a flurry of reviewing, and a reminder from an impatient editor that an article I'd promised was overdue kept me at my typewriter.

"I can't think why you stick with that old thing," Michael said as I put my faithful Olivetti back into its case. "You really ought to get a word processor."

"Oh, darling, I'm far too old to learn to use one of those things," I protested.

"Nonsense, Ma, they're perfectly simple."

Now that all solicitors' offices have become hi-tech and Michael has learnt to use the computer at work, he has assumed a superior air about things scientific that sits ill upon one who only scraped a

Pass in physics and chemistry in his O-levels at school.

"Look," he continued, "we'll get you a really *basic* one, one that even a child could use."

"Any child of five, nowadays," I said, "is more computer-literate than I will ever be."

"Yes, well, we'll get a nice simple one and I'll show you how to use it."

"Perhaps," I said, getting out the cloth and laying the table for supper.

"Oh, Ma, that's what you always say."

I went out into the kitchen to dish up, putting the radio on for the news, as I always do, only half listening as I drained the peas and put butter and nutmeg in the pan to glaze the carrots. I was just taking the fish pie out of the oven when I heard the words, "The death has just been announced of the composer Joshua Brendon. Mr. Brendon, who was sixty-four, was one of Britain's leading modern composers and wrote music for films and television. In 1990 he won an Oscar for his music for the film *Wuthering Heights*, and his musical version of *Vanity Fair* is still having a successful run on Broadway. Now here are the headlines again. . . ."

Automatically I switched off the radio and stood for a moment, unable to take in the fact of what had happened.

Michael, coming into the kitchen, looked at me with concern.

"Ma, what's the matter?"

"It's Josh, he's dead. I've just heard it on the radio."

"Oh, no, how awful! He was quite young. What did he die of?"

"I don't know, it didn't say. I must ring up Chillington and find out. Tomorrow, perhaps; I expect poor Mrs. Dawson—she's the housekeeper—will have enough on her plate. I expect the press will be onto it by now. One always forgets just how *famous* Josh is."

But before I got around to telephoning the next day, I had seen the morning paper with the details of Josh's death.

"Famous Composer in Shooting Mystery" was the headline in the *Telegraph.* I imagined those in the tabloids would be even more sensational.

Joshua Brendon, 64, the composer, was found dead on his estate yesterday. He had suffered shotgun wounds to the head. His housekeeper, Mrs. Margaret Dawson, 67, said that he had gone out for a walk in the early morning. "He often walked round with a gun before breakfast," Mrs. Dawson said, "to get the odd rabbit. When he didn't come back we were worried and one of the gardeners went to look for him." Mr. Brendon was lying by a gate leading into a small wood. His black and white spaniel, Flora, was still beside her master's body when he was found. Chief Inspector Eliot, of the Somerset and Avon police, said that investigations were being made and there would be an announcement in due course.

Then there were details of Josh's career, and the account ended:

> Mr. Brendon's wife, Alison, a former dancer with the Royal Ballet, died of cancer last year at the age of 52. There were no children.

The noncommittal tone of Roger's comment to the press made me certain that Josh's death might not have been an accident. I felt I really had to tell him what Josh had hinted about Graham—there must surely be some connection.

Somehow, perhaps because what I had to say was rather tenuous, I felt I'd rather ring Roger at home in the evening, so I tried to busy myself with routine household tasks (I couldn't manage work that required any sort of concentration) to get through the day. As I did some ironing, I turned over in my mind the possibility that whoever killed Graham could have wanted Josh out of the way because he knew something that might hold a vital clue to the murder. The motive, perhaps.

Alec Patmore had hinted that Graham knew things that might have been dangerous to someone else. I wondered if that was what Josh had wanted to tell me, and I cursed Mrs. Dudley for her inopportune interruption. The tablecloth I was ironing was too dry, so I got the sprinkler and damped it down. It occurred to me that perhaps Graham, in his capacity as solicitor, had found out something discreditable about one of his clients, something so bad that it had put his life in danger. It was possible. And, if that was so, then the murderer might be someone in London and I'd been on the wrong track altogether in limiting the suspects to the small circle of his friends. But was it possible that anyone outside that circle *could* have known where he was going to be and when? No, I was convinced that Graham's murderer was someone who knew him very well and not just a client.

For the rest of the day the problem kept going round in my mind until I could barely think straight. In despair, I put the dogs into the car and drove down to the beach to try and clear my head. The Promenade was crowded as the dogs and I picked our way through the visitors milling around—families with buckets and spades, beach-balls and ice creams, pensioners disembarking from their coach and making straight for the nearest café, and a solitary biker, his long hair straggling under his helmet, sitting motionless, a leather-clad mono-lith, astride his gleaming bike. I tried not to look at the shelter where Graham had died and walked quickly along the path by the sea that led to the fields beyond the town. It was quieter here, visitors preferring to keep to the beach and the harbor, and I met only the occasional dog-walker. There was a fresh wind coming in from the sea, agitating the scrubby tamarisks, just coming into bloom at the edge of the shore, and whipping up white foam onto the shingle.

Tris and Tess had found an interesting bush and

were investigating it minutely, so I sat down on one of the many seats that a benevolent council has provided for the largely geriatric population of Taviscombe. A seagull hovered nearby, fixing me with his bright and beady stare, wondering if I might be the source of food; but after a while he gave up and flew out to sea, shrieking disconsolately. Deprived of even this limited form of distraction, I returned once more to the thought of Josh's death.

"Better not to say it over the phone," he had said, whatever it was he had wanted to tell me; something that should not be overheard, something that might be damaging. To whom? To Graham, or someone else? *Had* Josh's death been an accident, or could it have been murder? I tried to remember what Peter had told me about safety catches on guns when he had first taken Michael out rabbiting and I had been going on, as mothers do, about was it safe, and was he *sure* Michael wouldn't let off the gun accidentally. . . . I would have to ask Michael. But a shooting incident is always open to a number of possible explanations. I needed to know more about the details of Josh's death before I jumped to any conclusions, and I wasn't sure how much Roger would be able to tell me. I shivered. The terrible fact of Josh's death swept over me, the sudden realization that I would never see Josh, sweet, kind Josh, again, and I felt ashamed that I had been thinking of his death in this way, just as part of a problem. I sat there on the seat, very still, and remembered him and mourned for him, while the gulls cried overhead and the waves broke monotonously at my feet.

Michael was out that evening. I had forgotten, and in the melancholy mood I was in, the house seemed very empty—even the presence of the animals couldn't dispel my sense of desolation.

When I felt I could wait no longer, I telephoned Roger and was lucky enough to find him in. I told him about my conversation with Josh and how it had been interrupted by Mrs. Dudley.

"Trust my grandmother-in-law!" he exclaimed. "Sorry, Sheila, do go on."

"So you see, I did wonder if there might be any connection between Josh's death and Graham's. If he *knew* something. You see what I mean."

"Yes," he replied slowly, "yes, I see." He was silent for a moment and then went on. "Actually, I can't tell you much about Joshua Brendon's death because we haven't had the path report yet. But it does seem to be a straightforward case of accidental shooting. He was out with his gun—he'd already shot one rabbit—and he was getting over a stile when it happened. He appears to have leaned his gun against the stile as he climbed over, but then he must have caught it somehow and it—well, it went off in his face."

"Oh, God!"

"So you see, it would have been difficult to murder someone in that way. Of course," he said on a sudden thought, "I suppose if he *knew* the murderer, they could have been chatting on either side of the stile, with the gun leaning up against it, and the murderer *could* have taken him off guard and shot him from that position. It's theoretically possible, though, honestly, not very likely. *If* that's what happened, then Brendon's fingerprints on the trigger would be smudged where the murderer's gloved finger was superimposed."

"I see."

It seemed wrong to be discussing Josh's death so coldly and clinically like this, as if it was some sort of puzzle we were solving as an intellectual exercise.

"The other possibility we usually have to consider in these rather ambiguous deaths is suicide."

My heart gave a lurch as I thought of Alison, and Josh's grief at her death. It was quite possible that he'd felt he couldn't live without her. "Living and partly living," he had quoted once. He put on a brave show, but I think we all realized that the light had gone out of his life, the mainspring of his existence had gone when Alison died. He may have decided that partly living was not enough.

"Was there any possibility that he might have taken his own life?" Roger asked. I hesitated, unwilling to expose Josh's grief to someone who hadn't known him, but Roger apparently had intended it as a rhetorical question and continued, without waiting for a reply, "Though why, if it *was* suicide, would he want to make it look like an accident?"

But that is just what Josh *would* have done—kind

and thoughtful even in death, he would want to spare his friends the distress of thinking that he'd taken his own life.

"Is there any way," I asked, "that you can tell if it was suicide and not an accident?"

"Well, now." Roger adopted a slightly schoolmasterly tone. "He was wearing a cartridge belt which he'd obviously filled up when he went out. Three cartridges had been taken from the belt when we found him. The rabbit he shot would have accounted for one, and the other two were in the gun—it was a double-barreled twelve-bore, quite an old gun."

"I think he told Peter once that the only gun he had belonged to his father," I said.

"Right. Well, then. One of the two cartridges in the gun had already been fired—we don't know what at, perhaps a rabbit that he'd missed—and the remaining cartridge was the one that killed him. We know that it was one of his own cartridges, fired from his gun, because we have the pellets from the body. Now, if it *was* suicide and he'd propped the gun up against the stile to make it look like an accident, then, in that position, he wouldn't have been able to pull the trigger with his finger, he'd have had to use his thumb. So if we find a thumbprint rather than a fingerprint on the trigger, then suicide would seem more likely."

"I see."

We were both silent for a moment, then Roger said kindly, "I know how distressing this must be for you, Sheila. Do try to put it out of your mind for a bit. I'll let you know as soon as we're more certain what exactly happened."

"Yes, thank you, Roger, I *will* try. But I was so fond of Josh. I'm grieving for him much more than I did for poor Graham. Is that awful?"

"Not at all. From what I can see, Brendon was a really good and remarkable person, while Graham Percy—well, I shouldn't be saying this, perhaps, but the more I investigate his death, the less sympathetic he becomes."

"Yes, Josh was so sweet and kind, as well as having all that wonderful talent, while Graham—I'm beginning to wonder how well we really knew him!"

There was a loud if muffled sound at Roger's end of the telephone line, and he said hastily, "Sorry, Sheila, I've got to go. Alex's crying and that's woken up Delia—Jilly's out at her Spanish class so I'll have to go and cope. All *right*, Delia, Daddy's coming! Sorry . . . I'll be in touch. Good-bye."

Roger was right. I must try and put the whole thing out of my mind. Resolutely I went back into the sitting room and put the television on. As I watched the two-dimensional characters in an American road movie slowly unfolding before me, I wished passionately that real life and the real people in it could be just as simple and uncomplicated, suffused in a golden glow of fictional happy ever after.

Foss jumped up onto my lap and began to knead

with his claws, pulling the threads of my skirt, which was his way of telling me that he was bored and wanted some food. With a sigh I got up, switched off the television, and reluctantly went back again into the real world.

· 13 ·

"I heard something today that might interest you," Michael said, washing his hands rather messily at the sink before supper a few evenings later.

"What did you hear? Oh, darling, you've splashed soap everywhere. I do wish you'd wash upstairs in the bathroom." Ignoring my strictures, Michael went on, "You know Martin's Uncle Giles?"

"Is that the one that's with that firm of solicitors in Holborn?"

"No, that's his Uncle George. This one's a big noise with a firm of accountants in the City." Michael's friend and colleague Martin has a plethora of relations who form a widespread and mutually dependent network in the legal and financial world. "His firm does a lot of work with Makepeace and Foster, Graham's old firm, so Martin pumped him a bit about things there. Well, he knew we'd be interested." He reached into the fridge and took out a can of beer. "Well, from what I can gather,

Makepeace and Foster is full of happy little campers now that old Graham's gone."

"Really?"

"It's not just that no one liked him very much—though they didn't—but he'd been with the firm for a very long time, and he'd accumulated quite a lot of information that various members of the firm would rather he hadn't."

"Information?"

"Let me put it this way. In any law firm, however well-regulated, someone, sometime, makes a right balls-up of some case or other. Usually they can smooth it over so that the client's none the wiser, but there's always a colleague who knows what's going on, and that colleague, as a result, then has a certain amount of influence, shall we say, over the person who made the balls-up; and he can rely on said person to back up any project he puts forward and expect them to help cover up any little mistakes *he* might make in his turn. As I say, Graham had been there a long time, he knew where an awful lot of bodies were buried—I'm speaking metaphorically, of course. At least, I hope I am."

"I see. And if he had this *influence*, then that might explain how he came to be a senior member of a prestigious firm when, as we all knew, he was a rotten lawyer."

"That and the fact that he had several important clients, which were his own, very special ones. Martin's Uncle Giles said that he always kept those very much to himself. No one else was allowed a sniff at them."

"The Shelleys and the Heywoods, for instance?"

"Yes. Oh, and Alec Patmore."

"Alec?"

"Apparently he handled the divorce for him."

"So it all sort of hangs together in a way—though I'm not at all sure in *which* way." I put a knob of butter into the cheese sauce and stirred it thoughtfully. "Of course, this might mean that someone in his own office had a motive for killing him."

"Yes, it's possible, I suppose. It all depends *what* sort of hold he had over people. Incompetence, perhaps, even a bit of sleight of hand with the cash somewhere, but I wouldn't have thought there'd be anything worth murdering for."

"Oh, well, it was just a thought. But it just goes to show. We simply thought Graham was a tiresome bore. We never really knew just what a nasty piece of work he was!"

The following Sunday was the christening of Jilly and Roger's son, Alex. "He's practically a toddler now," Rosemary said, "and much too big to fit into the family christening robe. Mother's furious about that, as you can imagine, but they had to keep putting it off because Roger's mother's been in Canada and they quite naturally wanted to wait until she got back. Anyway, it's after morning service at St. James' and then back here for a drink and something to eat. We've got rather more room than Jilly and Roger."

"How's the catering going?" I asked. "Is there anything I can do to help?"

"Bless you, no. I've got an enormous salmon to cook, and Mother's lent me Elsie." Elsie was Mrs. Dudley's slave and greatly renowned for her light hand with cakes and pastry.

"Oh, well, I'm sure everything will be delicious."

There were quite a few people in church. Far more than the usual morning congregation. Obviously, Mrs. Dudley had sent forth her fiat that all members of the Dudley family should attend. The only representatives of Roger's family able to be present were his mother and sister. A lesser woman might, perhaps, have been overwhelmed by the massed phalanx of Dudleys with their formidable leader, but Mrs. Eliot, as a former bishop's wife, was, I knew from experience, more than capable of holding her own.

It was a lovely day and the sun shone through the stained glass windows, bathing the aisle in blue and gold light. Rosemary, looking slightly distraught, came in with Jack and Mrs. Dudley, who was wearing a new and obviously fiendishly expensive summer suit and a hat closely modeled on those worn by the Queen Mother. Behind them were Jilly carrying Alex, and Roger leading Delia by the hand. I smiled at them as they passed up the aisle, and Delia, seeing a face she knew, stopped and said, "I've got new shoes on and if I'm good and don't make a noise I'm going to have a new dress for my Barbie doll."

She seemed inclined to expatiate on this theme, but Roger gave me a harassed smile and hurried her into the front pew next to Rosemary. Apparently this projected gift was sufficient to ensure Delia's silence throughout the service and, indeed, the actual christening itself. But Alex, too young to be amenable to bribery, gave a furious bellow when, at the moment of christening, the water dribbled down his head and neck, although the rector, in the marvelous words of the prayer book, had performed this task "discreetly and warily."

Rosemary had certainly provided masses of delicious food, and Jack was, as ever, assiduous in topping up people's glasses, so that the guests were soon circulating happily. Alex, affronted by the unexpected watery dip, had cried solidly all the way home and, now exhausted, was fast asleep in his cot; while Delia, having loudly claimed her reward for virtue, retired with it to the hall, where she sat on the bottom stair laboriously inserting her Barbie doll into what appeared to be a silver lamé jumpsuit.

I was amused to see that, intentionally or not, Mrs. Eliot had trumped the ace of Mrs. Dudley's new hat by wearing a plain all-purpose little number that had obviously done yeoman service at many ecclesiastical functions. It had the effect of making Mrs. Dudley look ever so slightly over-dressed.

"You are smiling a secret smile," Roger said. "Do tell me why."

I told him what I had been thinking and he laughed. "Now you mention it, you're right, of course. But what a subtle and feminine observation! How glad I am to be a mere male and not subject to such scrutiny!"

"Men are not exempt," I said. "Far from it. Anyway, it was a lovely service and everything went off very well."

"Yes, we're lucky that the new Rector is a member of the Prayer Book Society so we get the proper words."

"I know. I've actually started to go to church again. I hadn't been for ages—not since Mr. Huston introduced guitars into the service and wanted people to hug each other. He lost a lot of his congregation. Poor man, he thought the 'young people' would come, but of course they didn't. If they want rock music they go to a disco! And my generation, especially in places like Taviscombe, like things to be as they've always been. So we were all delighted when he went off to Coventry, and I should think he was quite relieved to be gone!"

During this little outburst, I was aware of having lost Roger's attention; he was fiddling with his glass and not quite meeting my eye. A faintly embarrassed silence fell between us, and then he said, "I know this isn't really the place to say this—look, let's go outside, I can't speak here." He turned and I followed him into the kitchen. He put his glass down on the draining board and said, "We've had the results of the postmortem. I think it's fairly certain that Brendon's death was an accident."

"Thank goodness," I said.

"A close examination of the gun confirmed it. Apart from the fingerprints being consistent with an accident—you remember, I explained about that—there were traces of bramble caught in the trigger."

"Bramble?"

"Yes. It seems most likely that he leaned the gun against the stile as he climbed over and then reached across to lift it over, but it was caught up in a bramble, and either he hadn't put the safety catch on properly, or it had slipped somehow—it was quite an old gun—and the action of lifting the gun set it off."

"How awful!" I exclaimed. "It just proves what Peter always said, that when you're out with a gun you must think about what you're doing every minute! Well, thank you for telling me what happened. It sets my mind at rest. I was so terribly afraid that poor Josh's death might have had something to do with Graham and I felt sort of responsible. Though I'm still left feeling a bit frustrated, not knowing what it was he wanted to tell me. Oh, well, I shall never know now."

"Not necessarily," Roger said.

I looked at him in astonishment. "What do you mean?"

He reached into his inside pocket and took out an envelope.

"After his death, when we weren't sure whether or not there had been foul play, we went through his desk. There were several letters there, obviously he had meant to post them. A couple were payments of bills, one was to his agent, and"—he gave me the envelope—"this was addressed to you."

I took the envelope, large and white and square with my name and address in Josh's familiar tiny, cramped handwriting squashed up in the center.

"Thank you," I said dully and put it in my handbag.

"There is just one thing, Sheila," Roger said tentatively. "I'm sorry—I have to ask—but when you've read the letter, could you let me know what was in it? I mean, in view of what you told me about Brendon and Graham Percy. . . ."

"Yes, of course," I said. "I'll let you know."

"What on earth are you two doing out here?" a voice behind us demanded. It was, of course, Mrs. Dudley. "Talking about *literature*, no doubt."

Mrs. Dudley did not approve of Roger's interest in literary matters. She didn't particularly approve of mine, though it might, perhaps, be acceptable as a suitable accomplishment for a female, rather like embroidery or crochet. Actually, what she didn't approve of was conversation in which she could not play a leading part.

She regarded us coldly, and I was amused to notice that Roger appeared to share my feeling of guilt, as if we were two naughty children found out in some misdemeanor. "Actually," she said (and no one can say "actually" with so much meaning as Mrs. Dudley), "I think you are required in the drawing room, Roger. That young friend of yours, the *journalist*"—a world of disdain in her voice for Lawrence, Roger's friend, one of Alex's godfathers, and a highly respected foreign correspondent on the *Sunday Times*—"was asking where you are. Apparently he and that young woman of his"—Lawrence's wife—"wish to take their leave. And why they only felt able to stay for such a short time on what *I* would have thought was such an important occasion . . ."

"It was very good of Lawrence and Rachel to come," Roger explained patiently. "Lawrence has to fly off to Sri Lanka tonight to report on the troubles there for his paper."

"Sri *Lanka*!" Mrs. Dudley exclaimed. "Whatever place is that to go to!"

"It used to be Ceylon," I said helpfully.

"I am perfectly aware of that, Sheila," Mrs. Dudley said repressively. "Not that I approve of all this chopping and changing of names all round the world. . . ."

"Right, then," Roger said, "if you'll forgive me, I'll just go and . . ." He turned at the door. "And, Sheila, you will let me know, won't you?"

"Yes," I promised, "as soon as I can."

"Let him know what?"

Mrs. Dudley never allowed good manners to stand in the way of her curiosity.

"Oh . . ." I tried to think quickly. "Nothing much. Just something he wanted me to ask Michael about the next clay shoot."

I could see that Mrs. Dudley didn't believe me, but she was too eager to tell me at great length about her disapproval of *all* the godparents and the general way the christening had been organized.

"I was very surprised that Roger's mother hadn't even bothered to buy a new *hat* for the occasion," she said, "and I thought Roger's sister looked positively *dowdy*. She'll never get a husband if she doesn't take a little more trouble with her appearance."

I made a noncommittal noise that might be taken for agreement, since I knew that it had not been thought politic to let Mrs. Dudley know that Roger's sister, Stella, enjoyed a loving and permanent relationship that neither partner wished to formalize with marriage.

"As for that friend of Jilly's—Anna, or whatever her name is—she looked most unsuitable in that long trailing skirt like a gypsy! Why they chose *her* to be that poor child's godmother, I shall never know! I told Jilly she should have asked her cousin Margaret, a really *nice* girl. I know her parents expected it and Winifred told me how disappointed she was."

Margaret, a second cousin actually, was a dull, lumpish girl, rather sullen and generally avoided by the family, as were her equally tedious parents. Mrs.

Dudley, too, had been used to speak slightingly of them, and they were only brought out now and displayed as desirable in order that Mrs. Dudley could be seen to know what was best in every situation. Deciding that she had set me right on a sufficient number of topics, she said briskly, "Well, we mustn't stand about here gossiping. People will be wondering where I've got to."

For a moment I stood there quietly in the kitchen, getting my breath back, as one always had to after any conversation with Mrs. Dudley. Then I opened my bag and took out Josh's letter. I turned it over in my hand, but I didn't open it. As Roger said, this wasn't the place. The letter seemed to be burning a hole in my bag, and I longed to get away so that I could see what was in it. Yet, when I got back home, I found myself curiously reluctant to do anything about it. I fiddled around in the kitchen, emptying the dishwasher and putting things away, making a cup of coffee that I didn't really want, even putting down extra dishes of food for the animals, to their surprise and delight. Eventually, when I couldn't put it off any longer, I went into the sitting room, took the envelope out of my bag, and opened it. The letter was typed, which was a relief, since Josh's handwriting wasn't easy to read.

My Dear Sheila,

Sorry I haven't been in touch before, but I had to stay in New York longer than I expected. Margot Bannister's taken over the lead in *Becky!*, and there were quite a lot of things that had to be seen to. And now I hear from Max that there's another panic, so I shall have to go back again next week. Ain't that the way! So I thought I'd better write it all down for you, since you must be wondering what on earth I was talking about when we were interrupted!

As you know, Graham Percy used to come to Chillington with Paul and Bryan and Alec in the old days. To be honest, I never really took to him, he wasn't my sort of person, I always thought of him as a bit of a hanger-oner, if you know what I mean. But he was their friend, and so I accepted him as such and tried to make him welcome. He didn't come with the others every time and it was noticeable that when he wasn't there—the atmosphere was quite different, they were much more relaxed and *themselves*.

One thing I did find pretty distasteful was that he tried to persuade me to let him represent me legally—contracts and things. I told him that my agent arranged all that, but he was quite persistent, and I think I would probably have not invited him again, anyway, even without the conversation I had with Bryan.

It was one of the times when Bryan came down on his own—he did sometimes. At that time he was going through a bad patch emotionally. He had this dreadful old mother, you know, terribly demanding and possessive, and he was terrified of her. He'd just met Odette and there'd been all sorts of trouble, as you can imagine. Anyway, he was in rather a fragile state when he came down and what with one thing and another, he got pretty drunk.

He went on a lot about his mother, of course, and then he started to talk about Graham. He said that Graham had mismanaged some legal affairs in a way that had cost him quite a lot of money. So I said, in that case why didn't he get rid of him, and he said he couldn't. At first, he wouldn't explain what he meant, but then he broke down and told me all about it.

Bryan and Paul had always been friends—they were at the same prep school—and when they met Alec at their public school they'd both taken to him at once. Graham tried to get into their group; he'd tagged after them, and although they kept on telling him to get lost, he still hung around. Anyway, he had a knack of making himself useful in some ways, so they more or less put up with him.

Their school was on the edge of Dartmoor, and a few miles across the moor there was an old wartime Army firing range. Of course it was strictly out of bounds, but as you can imagine, it held a great fascination for souvenir-hunting schoolboys because you could pick up spent bullets, bits of shrapnel, and tail fins and things. So, on a free afternoon, the three of them went off to have a poke around and have a smoke—just tobacco in those far-off innocent days!—in the old concrete pillbox there. Graham tried to join them, but they gave him the slip and were feeling very pleased with themselves.

They picked up a few bullets—it was just after the end of the war and there was still a lot of stuff lying around, though it was a bit rusty and corroded by then—and then Bryan gave a shout. He'd found a hand grenade under a gorse bush. Alec examined it and said there was no pin, but it hadn't gone off so it must be a dud. He threw it to Paul, shouting, "Catch!" and Paul threw it to Bryan, and they larked around with it for a while until they heard the sound of a tractor. The farmer whose land backed onto the firing range had caught them there once before and turned them off, warning them, with many oaths, what he'd do if he caught them there again.

The small tractor was approaching on the farm track some way below them, and Bryan, who had the grenade in his hand, said, "Let's chuck this at that miserable swine of a farmer—that'd give him a fright!"

Paul said, "Let me!," and snatched the grenade from him, but Alec said, "Here, give it to me—it'a too heavy for either of you clowns to throw that far!" and lobbed the grenade onto the tractor as it passed. They heard a thud and then a terrible bang which made them throw themselves onto the ground. After a bit they got up and saw the tractor on its side.

Alec started off down the hill to see what had happened to the farmer, but a second explosion, the petrol tank of the tractor, I suppose, stopped him in his tracks when the whole thing went up in a sheet of flame. Paul just stood there, absolutely petrified, but Bryan was really hysterical and gasping badly (he used to get dreadful asthma attacks if anything upset him).

Alec said, "There's nothing we can do—let's get out of here."

So, half-dragging Bryan, they got the hell out. But as they did so, Graham appeared. Apparently he'd been following them to find out where they'd gone, and he'd seen the whole thing.

The three were really frightened, terrified at what might happen if they owned up. But the farmer's death was assumed to be an accident—several people had already been killed on the moor by unexploded mortars—so they thought they were safe and tried very hard to put it out of their minds. Then Bryan started having nightmares, waking up screaming.

Graham, who was in the same dormitory, covered up for him, and they were all very grateful. But then, after a while, Graham began to make remarks, quite casually, about how dreadful it would be if anyone knew what had happened. And that was the beginning of it all.

As time went by and they all grew up, they realized more and more just what a horrendous thing it was they had done and what effect it would have on their lives (and their careers) if it should ever get out.

So that was Graham's hold over them. It *was* a terrible thing to have done, and I must say I was very shocked when Bryan told me, but they are all my friends, and it seems to me that they have paid quite a price for their crime, though you may not agree.

Anyway, Bryan begged me not to let the others know that he had told me about it, so I never have. I did try over the years to persuade Bryan to tell Graham to go to hell, but he never did. Apart from the fact that he was afraid it might affect the others, he's never told Odette, and I think he believes she might leave him if she knew. I'm sure Alec never told Julia, though I'm not sure about Paul and Alice.

So there you are. Since Graham was killed, I've been in two minds about what I should do. I couldn't quite bring myself to go to the police because that would betray the secret, and Bryan trusts me not to. I can't really believe, in spite of what they did that awful day, that Paul or Bryan could have deliberately murdered someone (Alec is obviously in no position to), but it does mean that if Graham was blackmailing them, then he could easily be turning the screw on someone else who *might* have killed him to shut him up. But I did feel that someone ought to know, and you seem the obvious person. I gather that you're friendly with the local copper who's doing the investigating. Perhaps you could just give him a hint. I (rather meanly) leave it to you.

Sorry we didn't have time for much of a chat. When I get back from New York we really will have that lunch date—and talk of pleasanter things than this.

Love to you and Michael,
Josh

Mechanically I folded the letter and put it back into the envelope. I felt overwhelmed by all the information I'd been given, and I didn't know what to do with it. I wished I could discuss it with Michael, but he was staying with friends for the weekend and wouldn't be back until late. I was moved, too, on a more personal level, by the letter from Josh. The knowledge that now we would never have that lunch together brought tears to my eyes. As always when I am distressed, I turned to the animals for comfort. I put the dogs in the car and drove high up into the hills.

We walked across the short springy turf, where the ling was coming into bloom and the young bracken was unfurling and the only sound was that of the wind in the high beech hedges that cut across the empty landscape. We walked until the sun started to set and barred the sky with pink and gold and purple and I was so tired that I knew I could go home and sleep and put off until tomorrow any thoughts of what I should do about Josh's letter.

· 14 ·

It's a funny thing how one day parents suddenly realize that their child has grown up. This may not occur until the child is well into his twenties, and although the mother (it's usually the mother) may still feel impelled to tell him (it's usually a son) for goodness sake to brush his hair and *do* please wear a sweater because it's really quite cold outside, nevertheless some incident or action will forcibly bring home to her that her child is now a responsible human being capable of mature thought and even advice. I can remember precisely when this happened to me—when Michael said that he'd been asked to be secretary of not one but *two* charity committees. It was quite a shock, believe me. But it was comforting now to know that when I put to Michael the problem of Josh's letter, I could expect a thoughtful and probably useful reply.

"So? What do you think?" I asked.

Michael handed the letter back to me.

"Well, it's fairly obvious what Josh wanted you to do."

"Tell Roger about Graham's blackmailing them, but not say why. I mean, what they did was a criminal offense, and I suppose they could still be prosecuted for it. *Should* be prosecuted for it, perhaps?"

"I'm not really sure," Michael said, "what the legal position would be. They'd have been about twelve or thirteen, I suppose, so it would have been a juvenile offense. Then it was, strictly speaking, an accident, and the verdict at the inquest was in fact brought in as such. Anyway," he concluded, "after all this time, if an allegation *was* made it would be more or less impossible to prove."

"True, still it wouldn't be fair to put Roger in the invidious position of having to cover up something like this." I put the letter back in its envelope and propped it up against the sugar basin. "Mind you," I said, "now that Paul's been eliminated it does rather point the finger at Bryan."

"Not necessarily. As Josh says, Graham may well have been blackmailing any number of people— that seems to have been the way he operated. And from what Martin's Uncle Giles said, we know that's what he did, in a minor sort of way, in the office. *We* can't investigate that side of things, but the police can."

I got up from the table to put another piece of bread in the toaster. "Of course," I said, remembering, "there was that message on Graham's answerphone."

"Which message?"

"The one from Bryan telling him to go to hell. Perhaps Josh's advice had finally got through to him and he was going to call Graham's bluff."

"In that case," Michael pointed out judiciously, "if he was going to face things out, he wouldn't have needed to murder Graham, now, would he?"

The bread shot out from the toaster, barely browned, and I put it back in again. "I don't know. Bryan is, as Josh said, pretty unstable. It might just have been a flash of bravado, on the spur of the moment, an impulse that he regretted later. And then he might have been afraid that Graham really *would* tell the world and decided that the only thing to do was to silence him forever!"

"It's possible. Still, for all we know, Bryan may have a perfectly good alibi, like Paul has."

"Yes," I said, brightening, "he might have."

Smoke and a smell of burning made me realize that the toaster had now trapped the bread in its maw and was incinerating it. I went over and switched it off.

"Don't bother about toast for me, Ma," Michael said, "I've got to go now. You phone Roger and tell him all about it."

I was occupying myself with various household tasks (some unnecessary), putting off the moment when I should take Michael's undoubtedly sensible advice, when the telephone rang. It was Roger.

"I thought you'd like to know," he said, "that they've released Brendon's body, and I believe the funeral will be the day after next, just family and close friends at the village church—so his cousin said."

"Oh, thank you so much for telling me. I'd like to go, of course. Though I suppose, because he was so famous and everything, there's bound to be a big memorial service for him up in London."

"Sure to be."

"Roger," I said tentatively, "about that letter . . ."

"Oh, yes, I was going to ask you about that. Was there anything relevant in it?"

"Well, in a way." I took a deep breath. "Something happened, years ago, when they were all at school together, something very—very *discreditable* that they were involved in. I'm afraid I can't tell you what it was because it was told to Josh in strict confidence—but Graham found out about it and he'd been blackmailing them ever since."

"I see."

"So, of course, if he's been blackmailing *them*, he could very well have been doing the same thing to all sorts of people we don't know about. In fact, Michael heard a whisper that that's how he managed to hold his position in his firm—though, of course, I don't know any *details*."

"Well, it's quite a thought. So now there are three motives for Graham Percy's murder."

"Well, not really, are there? I mean, Paul has an alibi, and, as for Alec Patmore, well, I saw him recently and there's no way he could have done it.

Which leaves Bryan. Have you spoken to him? Does he have an alibi?"

"Yes, I have, and no, he hasn't—well, not corroborated. Like most people, at that time of day he was having breakfast, but his wife was away, so there's no one to confirm it. He was in College, giving a tutorial at eleven o'clock, but I suppose there would have been time for him to have driven back to Oxford by then if he *had* killed Percy."

"I don't see him as a murderer, not Bryan. And, anyway, why kill Graham now, after all these years?"

"Something may have come to a head—I really don't know. Anyway, Sheila, thank you for telling me what you could about Brendon's letter. I'll make discreet enquiries in Graham Percy's office and see if I can come up with anything there."

"Good idea!" I said heartily, relieved that his attention had been diverted away from Bryan, for the moment, at least.

"I'll keep you posted," Roger said, "if there are any developments."

"I've got to the stage, with this wretched book, when I really ought to check a few things in the Bodleian," I said to Michael that evening. "Would you mind looking after things here if I went to Oxford for a few days?"

"And while you're in Oxford," Michael said sardonically, "you might just run into Bryan?"

"I might. In fact, I'll give him a ring and see if he and Odette would like to have dinner."

"What do you think you can possibly get out of him?"

"I don't know. I shall play it," I said vaguely, "by ear. So will you be able to get back at lunchtimes to see to the dogs, or shall I ask Rosemary to have them?"

"No, that's fine, I can get back."

"Oh good, I didn't really want to ask Rosemary because I think she's rather up to her eyes at the moment preparing for her mother's birthday lunch."

Mrs. Dudley's birthday lunch was a formal affair, rather along the lines of a state banquet, to which all her elderly friends and sycophants were invited with the express purpose of impressing them with the extent of her power and influence. Needless to say, it was Rosemary who bore the brunt of all the catering, administration, and entertaining, and Rosemary who bore the brunt of Mrs. Dudley's criticism and continual but conflicting instructions. It was an event dreaded by all (including the guests) except, of course, Mrs. Dudley, who liked to give the impression that she had organized the whole affair and cooked the elaborate five-course meal with her own hands.

When I rang Bryan he seemed quite pleased to hear that I would be in Oxford.

"It would be really splendid to see you, I can do with a bit of cheerful company. Odette's had to go back to France again. Her mother had a stroke, did

I tell you? That's why she was over there before, when Graham came to stay, and now Odette's sister, who was looking after her, has broken her arm so *she* can't manage. Heaven knows when Odette will be back! I'm sick to death of dining in College. Let's go to the Trout, for old time's sake. It's just down the road, so come and have a drink here first. I've got a couple of articles that I'd like to show you."

So that was all right. I was glad that Odette wouldn't be there—not that I've anything against her, she's really quite nice, but it would be easier to lead the conversation in the way I wanted it to go if I didn't have to make small talk.

When I was sorting out what to take with me (all the various medicaments I seem to need nowadays, comfortable shoes for sitting about in, layers of clothes because the weather's so uncertain, my little radio for *The Archers*, and several books to read, as well as those for work, in spite of Oxford's being full of bookshops), I discovered a library book that had secreted itself under the bed. In the way of all books that do this, it was one day overdue by the time I found it, so I was obliged to make a special trip to the library to return it.

While I was there I wandered round the shelves in my usual mindless way, hoping, as one does, to come upon some marvelous new author. In the theater section I noticed a biography of Alec Patmore and took it down. Leaning against the shelving I flicked through the photographs. There were several pictures of the young Alec, very lithe and athletic—playing tennis, in a sportscar, on a motor-bike, on a horse—which made his present immobility seem especially poignant. There was the debonair Mercutio and the quizzical Benedick and there the sardonic mask of Iago and the foxy glance of Volpone, all the great classical parts he had played as well as the occasional modern roles in *Private Lives*, *An Inspector Calls*, and *Daphne Laureola*. There were pictures, too, of Julia, her perfectly heart-shaped face, framed by a halo of dark hair, her great, gray eyes gazing out at the world with that mixture of innocence and knowingness that generations of theater-goers had found irresistible. Perhaps, in a way, it was right that she had died before that beauty had faded or that brilliance dimmed.

Usually when I go to Oxford I stay with my friend Betty, but this time I wanted to be free to concentrate on Bryan, so I booked myself into the Old Parsonage, a comfortable and mildly eccentric hotel on the Banbury Road. As I drove round the interminable Oxford ring road I tried to plan my conversation with Bryan, but since there was no way I could ask him outright any of the things I really wanted to know, this wasn't very profitable. So I switched the car radio on again and listened to a program about the horrors of E numbers in food, which, although deeply depressing, served to distract my mind from more immediate problems. That afternoon and the following day I spent dutifully in the Bodleian, and it was with a certain feeling of virtue that I drove out to Wolvercote in the evening.

Bryan's house is one of those rather pretty ones on the green, quite old and with roses and clematis growing in profusion over the front. He welcomed me enthusiastically and led the way through the house to his study at the back looking out over a pleasant walled garden.

"Sit down," he said, moving an unsteady pile of copies of *The Journal of Classical Studies* from a chair. "Sorry. Things get a bit out of hand when Odette's away. What will you have to drink? Gin and tonic? Fine. I'll just get it and then I'd like you to see these articles by old Matthew Philips. Remember him? He's been ga-ga for years now, but I really do think he's gone *completely* over the edge now! Why they made him Regius Professor I can't imagine. Quite extraordinary! He sent me these off-prints. . . . There now, is that all right? Enough tonic? Right then, where did I put them? Far too many *papers*— Ah yes, here you are . . ."

The telephone rang. "Oh, sorry, that'll be Odette; she usually rings at this time. Make yourself at home, I won't be long."

He went out of the room, shutting the door.

I leant across the desk to pick up the articles he had indicated, and as I did so, I knocked several of the papers that Bryan had been complaining about onto the floor. I had bent to pick them up and re-place them when my eye was caught by one of them, a white sheet of paper with a coat of arms in black—a police summons for speeding. I was able to identify it immediately because only the month before Michael had received just such a summons. ("But Ma, I was only doing forty-five, at the *very* most—on that last bit into Taunton. It was that day the car wouldn't start, and I was due in court at ten—one of those wretched camera things!") I looked at it, and to my surprise the summons was for the very day Graham was killed. The place was Fyfield and the time was nine-thirty a.m.

My first reaction was of surprise, Bryan not being the sort of person you'd associate with such a thing as speeding. Then, as I replaced the document on the desk (under some other papers so that Bryan wouldn't know I'd seen it), I tried to work out the implications of the time, the date, and the place. Fyfield is really quite near Oxford, so surely, when Roger asked him about his alibi, Bryan could have produced the summons as evidence that he was in Oxfordshire and not in Taviscombe at the time Graham was killed. Indeed, I seemed to remember an episode of *Columbo* that turned on just such an alibi. What reason could he have for not doing so? It's not as though a minor traffic offense would be harmful to his career.

Yet, as I considered the matter, I thought it might *just* have been possible to get from Taviscombe to Fyfield in two hours, early in the morning when the traffic was lighter, possible if one drove like a madman. After all, Bryan had received a summons for speeding.

The sound of the door opening made me snatch at the off-prints and try to appear engrossed in them.

"Odette sends her love, sorry to have missed you."

"How are her mother and her sister?"

"Her mother's much the same—I think it'll be a long job—but Françoise is managing to do a bit now, and they've found some old woman from the village to come in and do the housework, so it's not as bad as it was. Still," he concluded gloomily, "it's going to be a couple of weeks before she can come back."

As all his friends were aware, Bryan was deeply dependent on Odette and was lost without her.

"Couldn't you go out there?" I suggested.

He sighed and shook his head. "No, too much on here that I can't get out of. Now then, how about another drink, or shall we be off? I booked a table for seven-thirty. Take those off-prints with you. I'd really like to know what you think. It's a lovely evening, shall we walk?"

I have a great affection for the Trout at Godstow. As it did for so many undergraduates, it formed the backdrop to many happy (and often romantic) episodes in my youth. And (give or take a few minor changes) it has remained much as I remember it. The river still rushes dramatically by, the walls are still magically clad in wisteria, and the peacocks strut up and down, flaunting their brilliant plumage and uttering their raucous cries. And when Peter was alive and we visited the Shelleys, we always went to dinner at the Trout, so it has memories of a different kind for me, as well.

At first our conversation was of academic matters, but then Bryan spoke of Josh.

"I simply can't believe he's gone," he said. "A world without Josh seems almost too awful to contemplate."

"You were very close?"

"He was my best friend—he saw me through some really bad times."

"And so awful," I said, "that he went in such a tragic way."

"God, yes. The police are sure it was an accident?"

"Oh, yes."

"Only at first I did wonder . . ."

"I know. So did I, but Roger assured me that it really was a horrible accident."

"Thank God."

I pushed a floret of broccoli around my plate with my fork for a moment, and then I said, "He wrote me a letter the day before he died. The police passed it on to me."

"A letter?"

"Yes. The last time I saw him he was talking about Graham, and he said there was something he thought I should know, something important that the police might need to know that might help them catch his killer." I could sense Bryan's sudden tension.

"That's what the letter was about," I said.

"About Graham?"

"Yes."

"And was it important?"

"It might be. In a way."

Bryan picked up the bottle and filled up my glass.

"Are you going to tell me what it was?" he said, not looking at me.

"I think you can probably guess."

"Yes."

"Bryan. Look, Josh didn't want to betray your trust—or the trust of Paul and Alec, for that matter. He knew I would never say anything. And he knew that Roger Eliot (he's in charge of the case and a friend of mine) is very discreet and understanding. But he did feel that in a case of murder there are certain rules you must abide by, moments when nothing but the whole truth will do. Roger knows that Graham was blackmailing you all. He doesn't know why. And as for the blackmail—well, it doesn't mean that you're necessarily under suspicion."

Bryan gave me a quizzical look. "You don't think so?"

"Well . . ."

"Of course we are. The perfect motive. I'm sure your police inspector thinks that, however discreet he is. Graham was a mean-minded, slimy little sod, and the world is a better place without him. He's just about ruined my life, and I'm delighted that he's dead."

Bryan's voice rose and the two elderly Americans at the next table looked at him curiously.

The appearance of the waitress gave him a moment to compose himself.

"I don't think I want a pudding," I said. "It's such a lovely evening, shall we have our coffee outside?"

It seemed a good idea, since Bryan was obviously in a highly emotional state, to remove him to a less public place. I found a table by the river under a tree, away from the other tables and benches.

"This looks like a nice place," I said and sat down.

We sat in silence while the coffee was brought, and then I said, "I'd no idea that Graham was like that. I simply thought of him as a boring little man one was rather sorry for."

"Oh, no," Bryan said bitterly. "He was more than that. He was, I suppose, a fatal mixture of evil and incompetence."

"What do you mean?"

"He was our solicitor, of course, because of the hold he had over us, and then he managed our affairs so badly that we all suffered financially. And he stretched things out—poor Paul's tied up in some terrible boundary dispute that Graham was dragging on forever, and Graham was trying to make me appoint him as sole Trustee for my family's estate—he would have ruined me. Odette was beginning to ask questions. . . ."

"She didn't know? About Graham and what happened?"

"Christ, no. I couldn't bear it if she ever found

out—even after all this time! I was the one who found that bloody grenade. It was my idea to throw it. How do you think I feel about it? It gets worse as time goes on. It's my fault the others are in this mess." He put his head in his hands. "Josh said, call his bluff, he said Graham would never say anything now, after all these years. People would ask why he hadn't spoken before, they'd know he'd been blackmailing us. But I couldn't take the risk. If it ever got out, it would affect my position, and Odette— Odette would despise me." He raised his head and looked at me. "I expect *you* despise me, don't you?"

I shook my head. "I think that over the years you've all paid for what you did."

"God, yes."

"And now Graham's dead, perhaps you can put it behind you."

"Not if the police think we murdered him."

"Well, they know Paul didn't. He was on a train to London at the time of the murder—a friend of mine was on the same train. And Alec's in no state to travel, let alone kill anyone."

"So that just leaves me. I haven't an alibi."

"Where were you?"

"At home. Alone. Having breakfast."

"And no one saw you? The milkman, the postman?"

"No one."

I longed to ask him about the speeding summons, but of course I couldn't. I poured some more coffee into our cups.

"Actually," I said, "there were all sorts of dark goings-on at his office—the answer might easily lie there."

Bryan looked at me eagerly. "Do you think so?"

"The police are looking into it. Bryan, I wonder—Graham lost you and Paul a lot of money. Do you know if he did anything similar to Alec?"

Bryan shrugged. "I don't know. I think there was something about contracts in the early days, but then, when Alec became famous, his agent took care of all that side of things. Graham did handle the divorce; there may have been something about the settlement. I know Alec was furious with him round about then, but he never told me why."

"I see."

"We never ever mention it to each other," Bryan said, "what happened. Can you understand that?"

"Yes."

"It's as though if we don't talk about it, then it never happened. It makes it easier to live with oneself. . . . But sometimes, sometimes I do long to talk to someone, I wish that Odette knew. But I couldn't tell her, I couldn't risk losing her love and respect, she means so much to me. If she left me, I couldn't go on living."

There was a hysterical note in his voice, and I broke in hastily.

"You can always talk to me about it if you want to. You know that anything you say will go no further."

"Thank you, Sheila," he replied gratefully, "it

would help. In so far as anything can. I don't see how I can ever get rid of it all, one terrible thing after another. I can't really see any end to it."

I wondered if among the other terrible things that haunted Bryan there might be murder.

We sat in silence while the river rushed by over the little weir, and I wished fiercely that it could somehow carry all our problems, all our pain and regrets, with it.

· 15 ·

I thought I'd drive home from Oxford by way of Fyfield and the Vale of the White Horse. It was a pleasant route, and I thought I might as well see where the speed camera was. As I drove past the warning signs, carefully within the required speed limit, I saw the gray bulky shape of the camera on the other side of the road. If Bryan had been driving back from Taviscombe that morning, he might well have chosen this route rather than the Newbury way, since there would probably have been less traffic.

It was more or less lunchtime so I decided I might as well stop at the nearest pub. I pulled into the car park of the White Hart and was just locking the car door when a voice behind me exclaimed, "Sheila! Sheila Malory of all people!"

I turned round and saw Anne Watson, an old friend from Oxford.

"Anne! How lovely to see you. I'd forgotten you live round here."

Some of her friends thought at the time that it was a terrible waste when Anne gave up what would have been a brilliant academic career to marry a farmer. She was a very nervy, highly strung girl, and on the few occasions I had seen her over the years, I had come to realize that she had found a satisfaction and contentment in the hard physical work of the farm that she could never have had in the academic rat race.

"You look marvelous!" I said. And it was true. The glorious auburn hair was streaked with gray, and her complexion was weatherbeaten, but she had an air of cheerful serenity that was a pleasure to see.

"I'm on my way home from a few days in Oxford," I said, "and I was just going to have lunch. Can you join me?"

"Well, I've really just come out to collect some antibiotic from the vet, but Jim's not in today, so I haven't got to get back for anything. Yes, I'd love to."

We had a lot to catch up on, and it was only when we were drinking our coffee that Anne asked what I'd been doing in Oxford.

"Oh, just checking a few things in the Bodleian," I said.

"I do envy you," Anne said. "Still being in touch."

"It's nice in a way," I said, "and I've been grateful to have something like this to fill up my time since Peter died. But you've still got a very full life, with the farm and Jim and the boys."

"Yes, I suppose so—though Andrew is away at Agricultural College, and Robert's digging wells in Zimbabwe. But, of course, now I have the horses I suppose there really wouldn't be time for much else." Anne had recently taken up horse breeding in a modest way. "Still, one hankers—you know how it is!"

"It is," I said, "quite fun to be on the dustier fringes of academe, but when I see the sort of infighting that goes on nowadays, I'm truly grateful that I never made it my life!"

Anne laughed. "So did you see anyone in Oxford? Did you stay with Betty? How is she?"

"No, not this time. Anyway, I think she's off to New Zealand soon to see her new grandson. That's Harriet's second, and Tony and his wife have a little girl—I'm her godmother, isn't that nice? I do envy her having all those grandchildren. Michael, alas, shows no sign whatsoever of settling down. No, the only person I saw was Bryan Shelley. I can't remember, do you know him?"

"Bryan? Yes, I do. I'm secretary of our local history society and he sometimes comes down and talks to us. Actually," she said laughing, "a really incredible thing happened a little while ago."

"Really?"

"You know that our farm is quite near Uffington."

"Near the White Horse?" This is a famous landmark, the figure of a horse cut into the chalk of the hillside by primitive people.

"Fairly near. Anyway, it's quite a rich area archaeologically. Jim's very interested, and he's given permission for a couple of digs on our land."

"How lovely to have something like that right on your doorstep!"

"Well, one morning I'd gone out very early to check on one of the mares. She'd had a touch of colic the day before, and I wanted to see that she was all right. I saw to the mare and decided to walk back across the fields. It was a lovely morning and I was just enjoying being out, because we'd had several days of rain, when I saw this man. He was crouched over something, moving backwards and forwards across the field, and I must confess, I was really quite frightened. Then I saw that he was using a metal detector."

"Good heavens!"

"I was really annoyed. I mean, you know how disruptive it is to any archaeological dig to have some idiot fooling around with one of those things and disturbing potential sites!"

"Of course."

"I shouted at him and he turned round, and— guess what!—it was Bryan Shelley!"

"No!"

"I couldn't believe my eyes! He was tremendously embarrassed. Well, you can imagine! Deighton Professor of Classics *and* a highly respectable member of the Archaeological Society!"

"What on earth was he doing?"

"Apparently it's become an obsession with him."

"Ah," I said. "That explains it."

Bryan's obsessions are a long-standing joke among his friends. He takes up some new interest—bridge, pottery, stamp-collecting, model soldiers—and immediately it becomes a consuming passion to which he devotes every available minute (apart from his work) of his waking day. We often wonder how Odette puts up with it, though I believe she came very near the limit of her patience when he filled the house with tropical fish. Fortunately these crazes aren't long-lived. Once he has built up his passion for the latest one to a white-hot heat, he quickly loses interest.

I explained this to Anne, who laughed and said, "I'm relieved to hear you say so. I mean, I wouldn't say anything, and fortunately Jim just thought it was funny, but if anyone else got to know about it, it wouldn't do his academic reputation much good. Actually, I did say that he could use the thing on our land if he liked, so I do sometimes come across him if I'm out early in the morning."

"Bryan always was a bit odd," I said. "Still, as you say, it's just as well no one else knows about it."

"He was very agitated that morning," Anne said. "Actually, he told me later that he was so upset that, going home, he was driving too fast and got caught by the speed camera at Fyfield."

"What!" I exclaimed.

Anne looked at me in surprise.

"Look," I said, "can you, by any chance, remember *when* it was? The morning you caught him."

"Well, yes, actually, I can. It was the twenty-fourth of last month. Jim's birthday, so, of course, I can remember. But why on earth do you want to know that?"

I felt I knew Anne well enough to be able to confide in her, so I explained about the murder (though, naturally, I didn't mention the blackmail) and told her, in general terms, about Bryan's need for an alibi.

"Oh, well," she said, "he was here just after eight o'clock that morning. When did you say this person was killed?"

"Around seven-thirtyish."

"Oh, well, there's no way Bryan could have done it, then."

"No, absolutely not. And, of course, he couldn't really say where he was because it would look so bad if it got out! Silly old thing! He really does get himself into impossible positions, he always has. We've often thought it was just as well he and Odette never had children, it must take all her time to look after him!"

When I got home I passed my information on to Roger, who laughed and said, "No wonder he was reluctant to claim an alibi. Oh, well, that eliminates him. Back to square one."

"Have you any sort of lead?" I asked tentatively.

"To be honest, no, we haven't. Actually, we're rethinking the possibility that Graham Percy was mugged."

"But the wallet, just thrown away like that . . ."

"I know. But perhaps whoever it was didn't actually mean to kill him. He might have just threatened him with a knife and then Percy moved suddenly and the knife slipped and that was that. Then the assailant panicked and threw the wallet away. He'd have known that if he'd kept anything we could have traced the murder back to him."

"Well, it is a possibility, certainly. Do you have any local suspects in mind?"

"A couple. And then there's the biker that someone saw on the Promenade around the time the murder must have been committed."

"Really?"

"A woman who lives in one of the cottages on the quay was looking out of her bedroom window and saw this person on a motorbike coming from that end of the Promenade round about the time in question. It's a pity it was a woman, a man might have been able to tell us what make of bike it was. That might have been a help. Still, we're checking all the local lads, just in case."

"Well, really," Michael said, when I told him later what Roger had said. "If you think about it, it must be something like that. I mean, you haven't any other suspects left."

"No, I suppose I haven't."

I tried to put the whole thing out of my mind. Let Roger work it out, there was nothing I could do now. Besides I had my work to catch up on.

A few days later, I was just trying to sort some of my Bodleian notes with a view to getting on with my long-overdue article on Charlotte M. Yonge and Keble, when the phone rang. It was David.

"Sheila, darling, could you do me an *immense* favor?"

"If I can."

"Could you possibly go to Bath and collect a letter from Alec for me?"

"A letter?"

"Yes, it's the provenance for one of the items he lent—no, *gave* me for the exhibition. He forgot to put it in with the other things, and quite honestly, I really wouldn't like to trust it to the post. I don't need it immediately, so whenever you come down to Stratford will do, but Alec seems to want to get everything sorted straight away. So—*would* you mind terribly?"

"No, that's fine. I'd be delighted. Actually, it would be interesting to see Alec again."

"Marvelous."

"What's the item?"

"A feather."

"A *feather*!"

"I know, it does sound odd. But it's the feather Irving used in *Lear*, you know, Act Five, Scene 3, when he's bending over Cordelia's body. 'This feather stirs, she lives!' You must remember that marvelous story of Graham Robertson's about how Irving was by the sea of Boscastle, studying that scene, which is set by the sea, and said, 'Where am I going to get the feather?' and then saw that the cliffs were covered with feathers from seabirds."

"And this is one of them?"

"That's right. And the letter was from Irving's stage manager, I forget his name, to Alec's grandfather, sending him the feather as a souvenir of the performance."

"How lovely! Goodness, don't you wish film had been invented then? Think of being able to *see* Irving's Lear and Ellen Terry's Cordelia!"

"Did you know that before Irving bent to pick up Cordelia's body he spat on his hands and rubbed them together, just like a laborer. A throwback, perhaps, to some Cornish farmer ancestor!"

I laughed appreciatively. "How can Alec bear to get rid of all those splendid theatrical objects?"

"I don't know," David said. "Perhaps he's iller than he lets on. I must say, I thought he looked dreadful when we saw him. He'd suddenly become a really old man."

"It's terribly sad."

"Mind you, he's never been the same since Julia left him."

"What happened there?" I asked curiously.

"We never really knew. It was a bit odd, really. I mean, it was a fairly turbulent marriage, terrific scenes and one or other of them flinging out in a rage, but I'd have said that, through it all, they were tremendously in love."

"She went off with someone else, though?"

"Yes, young Vivian Simon, but it was only a fling.

It had happened once before—years ago, with Toby Whipple—but we were all sure she'd come back to Alec. But instead of that, divorce! Incredible! She never married him—Vivian, that is. And then she was dead. I'll never forget Alec at her memorial service. He read, 'Fear no more the heat of the sun,'— God, she was a *wonderful* Imogen—and halfway through, he just broke down. It was terrible."

"Understandable, though."

"Oh, yes, but when I saw him after, all he could say was, 'She would never forgive me for being so unprofessional.' He was white as a sheet and shaking. I don't think he's ever been himself, mentally or physically, ever since."

"Poor Alec," I said softly.

"It's funny, though," David said, "now I come to think of it. There was something very strange about that divorce."

"What do you mean?"

"Well, I saw quite a bit of Alec round about then. We were both in *End Papers,* that rather trendy thriller Sam Glenn directed, do you remember? And you *know* what dreadful longeurs there always are in filming. So we had quite a few chats—well, we were the only two theater people, so we rather clung together! Anyway, as I say, I was around when all this was happening. Alec was upset, of course, at Julia going off like that, but I'm sure he was positive she would come back to him. Even when the divorce proceedings started, he didn't really seem concerned. Not because he didn't care, no, it was as if he didn't really take it seriously."

"How odd."

"Well, yes and no. Alec and Julia had this very peculiar relationship, almost as if they were playing a game together, a game that only they knew the rules of. It was as if they enjoyed living on a sort of knife-edge."

"Goodness!"

"I know. *I* wouldn't care to live like that, but they seemed to thrive on it. Right up to the last minute Alec seemed unconcerned, so that when the divorce was actually made final, he went to pieces. I suppose he never really believed she'd go through with it. He was desperately upset for a few weeks, and then one morning I saw him in makeup—it was some ghastly hour of the morning when no one looks their best, but Alec looked appalling. I asked him if he was all right, and he made some really *savage* comment, really hurtful. After all, I was only concerned about him. Then he apologized and said that he'd just had some bad news. I asked if he wanted to talk about it and he said he didn't. Later on, when we were waiting for them to set up a tracking shot—that sort of thing always takes ages—he went off and I overheard him talking on the phone. He was saying, 'Do you mean to tell me, Graham, that *you* were responsible . . . ?' He sounded absolutely furious. Then he saw me and broke off. He was dreadfully agitated, so I made myself scarce. But I imagine, don't you, that your

friend Graham was somehow involved. He was
handling the divorce, after all."

"How extraordinary!"

"And then, of course, a short time after that, Julia
was killed in that crash and young Vivian, too. He
wasn't a bad actor, you know. His Hamlet was
dreadfully superficial, he wasn't really up to it, but
he was quite excellent as Konstantin in *The Seagull*
at the National the year before."

"Yes," I said absently. "I saw it."

"Oh, well," David said, "all water under the
bridge, I suppose. So I'll tell Alec you'll be collecting the letter? Though perhaps you'd better give
him a ring yourself to arrange a time. It *is* good of
you, darling, but I'm really up to my eyes with this
exhibition, and Beth's coming over from Australia
especially for it and she *is* the founder of the feast,
as far as the Institute's concerned, so I want it to be
very special. I mean, she's an absolute sweetie—I'm
sure I told you—but definitely beady-eyed, so I
need to spend every possible minute getting it
right!"

After David had rung off I sat for quite a while
thinking about what he had said. It would seem that
Alec Patmore also had a reason to hate Graham.
Presumably it was something to do with the divorce, though I couldn't imagine what. But Graham
had obviously done something wrong, something
that had upset Alec a great deal, that had, in effect,
ruined his life. So now it seemed that Alec might
have had a motive for Graham's murder.

But that was no good. I'd seen for myself that Alec wasn't physically capable of murdering anyone. But, it suddenly occurred to me, there was someone who was utterly devoted to him, who might perhaps have been the instrument he could use for his revenge.

· 16 ·

I telephoned Alec the next day and got Penrose.

"Oh, yes, dear, Mr. Beaumont's just rung. So when would you like to come?"

"Would Tuesday be all right?"

"Just a sec. I'll go and ask *him*. He's just having his breakfast."

"Oh, I'm so sorry. Is this an inconvenient time?"

"No, dear, don't apologize! It's just that he had a bad night last night so everything's a bit behind this morning. Hang on, I won't be a minute."

I heard a murmured exchange in the background, then Penrose said, "Okeydoke. That'll be fine. *He* says come to lunch."

"That would be lovely, thank you."

"About twelvish then. It'll be a treat to cook for someone who enjoys their food—*he* only picks at things now. I'll do you my sole Véronique, shall I? And a Queen of Puddings—my specialty!"

He gave a shrill laugh, and I suppressed a giggle

and said, "That sounds heavenly. I shall look forward to it very much."

I met Rosemary in the supermarket car park, trying to retrieve the pound coin from her trolley.

"These wretched things! I can never get the money out, and when I go and get a lad from the store to do it for me, it comes out straight away and he looks at me pityingly, as if I were ninety-five and mentally deficient!"

"I know. The horrors of modern living!"

Rosemary gave a great shove, and the coin fell to the ground.

"I'm glad I bumped into you," she said, bending to retrieve it. "I wanted to ask if you could possibly come and give me a hand next Tuesday or Wednesday to address some envelopes and see to those leaflets for the appeal for St. James's. In a rash moment I took the thing on, and what with the christening and one thing and another, I haven't got round to it and the committee meeting's on Friday and I daren't *face* Beryl Mathews if it isn't done. You know what she's like!"

"Sure," I said. "Wednesday I can manage. I'm going to Bath on Tuesday."

"Oh, bless you! What are you going to Bath for? Shopping?"

"No, I'm going to see Alex Patmore to get something from him for David. He's invited me to lunch."

"Oh, lucky you!" Rosemary said enviously. "I al-

ways thought he was immensely glamorous. We
were mad about him! Do you remember? And that
time when we cut sports day at school and sneaked
off to London to see a matinee of *Romeo and Juliet*!
And then the train was late and it was nearly ten-
o'clock when we got back to Taviscombe. My
mother was furious and wouldn't let me go out anywhere for ages, but it was worth it!"

"Goodness yes, I'd forgotten that! He *was* gorgeous then, wasn't he?"

"They both were. She was so beautiful. I can always remember the sort of *electricity* between them.
Fantastic! Extraordinary that they split up like that,
I could have sworn it was a till death do us part sort
of thing. Still, I suppose these things happen, especially in the theater."

"And now she's dead and he's a crippled old
man," I said sadly.

We both considered this thought for a moment,
and then Rosemary said briskly, "Well, I'd better be
off. I've got to collect Delia from nursery school."

"Is she enjoying it?"

"Loves it. And guess who gets to give out the ap-
ples at break-time! A born milk-monitor, if ever I
saw one, bossy little thing. She'll be running the
country by the time she's twenty-one."

Remembering that matinee of *Romeo and Juliet*
and our schoolgirl crush on Alex Patmore, I ago-
nized even more than usual, on Tuesday, over what
to wear. I finally decided on a silky black and white
print dress (what my mother used to call a garden

party frock) and a black jacket, and although I proposed to drive in my comfortable flat-heeled shoes, I took a more elegant pair with me in a bag, to change into when I arrived.

I left very early because I intended to go the long way round to Bath, by the minor roads, to avoid the hassle of the motorway. As I drove, I became increasingly nervous, partly because one does, really, when going to have lunch with someone quite famous, but partly because I had this uneasy feeling at the back of my mind that perhaps I might be about to find out something I didn't really want to know about Graham's murder.

The fact was that Penrose (did he have no Christian name? I wondered) had devoted this latter part of his life to looking after an irascible invalid, not out of habit, or for money, or even a sense of duty, but from what could only be a kind of love. What he was prepared to do because of that love, I didn't know; and because I had found Penrose entertaining and touching in his loyalty, I quite honestly didn't want to know.

There was something else, too, niggling away at the back of my mind. Something that had happened on my last visit to Laura Place. Whether it was something that had been said or something I had seen I didn't know, but there was this *feeling* that something was wrong, and it was important to find out just what it was.

There was very little traffic, and I got to Bath far too early. I found a space in the car park, changed into my high-heeled shoes, powdered my nose and renewed my lipstick, looked despondently at my hair in the mirror, and wondered what to do. I could wander round Bath for a bit, but my shoes weren't really comfortable enough for walking very far up and down hilly streets, and besides, the sky was overcast and it looked like rain, so I didn't fancy that. Nor did I feel like sitting in the car for half an hour, getting more and more nervous. I decided to risk being impolitely early.

Penrose, answering the door, looked slightly put out, as well he might, but he quickly recovered his equanimity and welcomed me in.

"I do apologize," I said, "it's really unforgivable to be so early, but the traffic was very light, and I always leave far too much time to get anywhere, and I really didn't feel like sitting in the car for half an hour. . . ."

"Oh, I *know*, dear. I'm always too early for everything, spend *hours* waiting. Still, I always say, better too early than too late! *He's* still upstairs. It takes him a while to get ready and he won't let me shave him. I'll just pop up and tell him you're here. Would you like to keep me company in the kitchen while I finish off? Here we are. Won't be a sec."

"Do give Sir Alec my apologies for being so early and tell him please not to hurry."

"Okeydoke."

Trinculo was occupying what I took to be his usual chair, so I sat down in the other and awaited Penrose's return. He wasn't long.

"He'll be a little while, so you're to have a G and T, if that's just what you'd like?"

"Just a small one would be lovely," I said.

Penrose put quite a lot of ice in a tumbler, added gin and a twist of lemon. "Help yourself to tonic, dear." He put the bottle beside me on the table. "There's a nice bottle of Bouvray in the fridge to go with the sole. I know it's not a *fashionable* wine, but it's one *he* always likes with fish."

"It sounds delightful," I said.

"Well," Penrose said, pouring himself a rather larger gin, "this is cosy! Nearly everything's done, I've only got the sauce to make."

"I hope Sir Alec had a better night last night," I said. "When I phoned, you said that he hadn't been sleeping well."

"No, well, sometimes it's worse than others. Just as well *I'm* a light sleeper"—he tossed his head and the gold chains round his neck swung from side to side on his black sweater—"seeing as how *he* calls out for me to make him a hot drink when he can't sleep."

"It does sometimes help," I said. "When my mother was ill I used to make her some Horlicks, and that usually sent her off."

We continued with this theme for a while, and as I watched Penrose's long fingers skillfully peeling the grapes for the sole Véronique, against my will I found myself wondering if those hands might just have plunged a knife into Graham Percy. I thought

I'd better start the conversation again to put such thoughts out of my mind.

"My friend Rosemary and I were remembering when we played truant from school to go to a matinee of *Romeo and Juliet*," I said. "That must have been in 1959! Were you with him then?"

"Oh, yes, that was at the Old Vic, wasn't it? If you could have seen the dressing rooms in those days! Shocking, they were, even the Number One—no room to swing a cat! Just as well it was such a short season. They took that production to America after three months. But you're wrong—it was '60, not '59."

"Surely not, it was just after we'd taken our School Certificate exam, and I'm sure that was '59."

"Oh, no, dear. I'm positive it was '60. It was Madam's twenty-fifth birthday during the run, and I made this cake with silver decoration, silver for twenty-five, you see. Quite a tour de force, if I do say so myself!"

"It sounds lovely. But I could have sworn it was '59."

Penrose wiped his hands on a tea towel. "Tell you what," he said. "I'll find the program, that'll settle it!"

"Splendid."

"They're just outside in the garage—there're filing cabinets full of them."

I got to my feet. "Can I come and look?"

"Yes, it's just through here. Mind those sacks of compost. I'm just planting out my busy lizzies."

He led the way through the back door, across a little patio, and into the garage.

It was large, big enough for two cars, though in fact there was only one (a fairly new Rover), and one wall was, as Penrose had said, lined with gray filing cabinets. There were also several tea chests with a pile of framed playbills leaning up against them. Next to them was a large object covered with a sheet.

Penrose opened one of the filing cabinets and started to look through the folders.

"They're *supposed* to be in alphabetical order—ah, here we are. Well, would you believe it, you're right, dear. Opened May 1959. Oh, of course, now I remember! Madam's birthday *was* during the run, but it was when we were in New York. That's right, because he took her to Sardi's after the performance and the band played 'Happy Birthday to You' as they went in (they did that sort of thing at Sardi's, you know), and Madam had on this simply *gorgeous* dress, from Bergdorf's, oyster satin, cut on the cross, really gorgeous, I'll never forget!"

His voice trailed away, and he stood leaning on the filing cabinet, holding the program in his hand.

"You must both miss her very much," I said.

"Yes." He spoke very softly. "Things were never the same after she went. Not for him or for me. And then . . ." He crumpled the program in his hand in a passionate gesture.

"I'm so sorry."

At the sound of my voice he seemed to be aware

once again of his surroundings. He looked down at the program, smoothed it out, and put it back in the drawer.

To cover the embarrassment of the moment I went toward the stack of playbills and examined them.

"These are fascinating," I said. "*An Inspector Calls* at the Garrick, *Man and Superman* at Wyndhams. And, oh look, here's *Volpone*. I remember seeing that at the Aldwych."

"That was another terrible theater!" Penrose seemed to have recovered his equanimity. "No hot water half the time! And freezing cold! I said to *him*, it's all very well for you, on stage under a fur rug on a great big bed, done up in all that velvet, and there's poor me shivering with cold backstage!"

I put the playbills back against the tea chests and turned to face him. As I did so my heel caught in the corner of the sheet shrouding the object in the corner and it fell away, revealing a motorbike.

"Goodness!" I exclaimed. "Isn't that a beauty!" I looked at the name on the tank. "A Norton, isn't it?"

Penrose turned round from the filing cabinet.

"Yes, that's right," he said. "Like the one Sir Ralph had. They used to race each other sometimes. . . ."

"It's very big," I said, "quite heavy to handle. My son, Michael, would be fascinated by it. He's mad about motorbikes, though he could only run to a small Honda."

"Oh, he loved it," Penrose said. "Wouldn't get rid of it, even when . . ."

"Yes, I can understand that. Do you ever ride it?"

There was something like fear in Penrose's eyes as he gave his shrill laugh.

"Me, dear? Not on your life! You wouldn't get me on one of those things, not with my vertigo!"

I bent down and looked at the machine more closely. It was very well kept, the chrome was bright. But the underside of the flaps were covered with dried mud. Red dried mud. I ran my hand over the raised metal letters on the black tank, and as I did so I felt something slightly tacky under my fingers, which I recognized as the sticky residue from a lime tree. There are lime trees along part of the Promenade at Taviscombe, and as I know to my cost, any car (or motorbike) left under them be-comes coated with the stuff.

Penrose crossed to my side and covered the bike up again. He looked at me steadily for a moment, then he said, "That sole will be dry as a bone if I leave it much longer," and led the way back into the house.

· 17 ·

I sat down again in the kitchen and took up my glass. The ice had melted by now and the remaining gin was very diluted, but I felt I needed some sort of stimulant, however weak, to help me pull myself together. Obviously that motorbike had been ridden fairly recently. The red mud (surely the mud round Bath wasn't red?) hadn't been cleaned off nor the sticky lime tree sap. I wasn't sure if Penrose had seen me noticing these things. Certainly he had been disconcerted when the sheet had fallen off and the motorbike had been revealed. I looked at him carefully. He seemed wholly absorbed in stirring the cream sauce, but I thought there was a kind of tension in the way his shoulders were hunched. His voice, however, was perfectly normal when he said, "Another G and T, dear?"

"No thanks, this is fine."

"Rightyho. This is nearly ready." He took the pan

off the stove and said, "I'll go and see how he's getting on."

He went out of the room, and I tried to make some sort of sense of the jumble of thoughts and speculations whirling round in my mind. Alec Patmore appeared to have a motive for murdering Graham. Because of Graham's habit of informing everyone about his movements, Alec would have known where his victim would be. Penrose, who was devoted to his master, could easily have ridden the bike down to Taviscombe early that morning, waylaid Graham, stabbed him, taken the wallet to make it look like a mugging that went wrong, and then gone back to Bath without anyone's being the wiser. It all fitted together perfectly well, but somehow something didn't seem right. There was still that nagging feeling that I'd missed something important.

As it so often does nowadays when I'm agitated, I felt my face getting hot and red, signs of increasing age, I suppose. I took my compact out and applied a liberal amount of powder. My expression in the mirror looked almost distraught, and I tried to compose myself.

"There now, *he's* on his way down, so come along into the dining room." Penrose came back into the room, and I hastily put my compact away and got to my feet.

The dining room was handsomely furnished, with an elaborate chandelier hanging over the fine mahogany table. Two places were laid, one at the head, where there was no chair, and one at the right-hand side. The cloth and table napkins were white, heavy damask, and the china was white and gold. Surprisingly, in the center of the table was a large silver gilt epergne, around whose sides wolves and wild boars stalked each other. There also appeared to be some sort of script running around the base, but I was unable to read it since the room was really quite dark. As it was now raining quite heavily outside and the sky was dark, I was surprised that Penrose hadn't put on any lights. Still, I could understand that perhaps Alec preferred not to have the signs of illness and aging cruelly exposed.

The door opened and Alec Patmore came in. He neatly maneuvered his wheelchair into place at the head of the table and applied the brake.

"Do sit down," he said. "I'm so sorry to keep you waiting."

"No, really, it was unforgivable of me to arrive so early."

He caught sight of the epergne and gave a groan. "Oh, God, that bloody monstrosity! Penrose *will* do it! Penrose!" he roared as his dresser came into the room. "What the devil do you mean by putting that *thing* on the table?"

Penrose slid a plate of sliced avocado, tomato, and mozzarella in front of each of us.

"*I* think it looks nice. Anyway, we hardly ever have anyone to lunch nowadays so I thought I'd give it an airing." He turned to me. "They gave him that in Russia, when he did *The Tempest* at the Moscow Art Theatre."

"It's very—er—handsome," I said.

"It's totally misbegotten," Alec said. "Take the bloody thing away, it puts me off my food."

Penrose gave an audible sniff and removed the epergne.

"Well, I think it gives the place a bit of tone," he said going out of the room.

I smiled at Alec, but somehow I felt that this had been a contrived incident, a little bit of byplay put on for my benefit, though why I couldn't imagine.

"Poor Penrose," he said, "he misses all the entertaining. He adores cooking, and I—well, I don't take much interest in food nowadays."

I asked him about his tour of Russia, and throughout lunch we talked about the theater.

"It really was the golden age, wasn't it?" I asked. "From the forties up to the seventies. I'm glad I lived through it. There'll never be another time quite like it."

"The star system, you mean? Larry and John and Ralph, Edith and Vivien and Peggy? Certainly things are different now. Not, I think, better, not for the theater. The stature has gone."

"And the glamour," I said.

"Television has cut us all down to size. It isn't easy now to be larger than life." He laughed lightly. "Not my style. Just as well I got out when I did."

"Do you miss it?" I asked.

"In a way. I miss the actual *being* in a theater, the

audience out there. That space between the stage and the auditorium and how, just occasionally, you can cross it! As for the rest, the acting . . ." He laughed. "Whatever we do is acting in a way. All of us. Don't you agree? We all hide ourselves behind a mask, keep back something of our real selves, put on a performance. . . . Don't you think?" He looked at me quizzically, and I tried not to catch his eye.

Penrose came in.

"I've put the coffee in the drawing room," he said, opening the door. Alec deftly spun his wheelchair round away from the table and waved me ahead into the drawing room. Penrose poured the coffee.

"That was a really delicious lunch," I said to him. "There was something extra in that sauce with the sole, surely?"

He looked gratified.

"Pernod, dear. Makes all the difference, doesn't it?" He whisked a plate of petit fours in front of me, said, "Give me a shout if you want anything," and went out.

Alec twirled his chair round to face me, and for some reason, there was something familiar about the way he did it. Suddenly it came to me. "*Daphne Laureola*," I exclaimed.

He looked at me in surprise.

"That's how you did it in *Daphne Laureola*, when you played the old man in the wheelchair!" I said.

He raised his eyebrows. "How kind of you to remember."

"I'm sorry, I shouldn't have said . . ."

"Not at all. You are quite right. Playing that part was useful practice. I became quite adept at managing a wheelchair—especially difficult on stage, you know. And you see how handy it has been, very much like riding a bicycle, one never forgets."

"Or a motorbike. My son would envy you that beautiful Norton!"

"Ah, yes." There was just a flicker of hesitation before he replied, and I knew that Penrose had told him that I'd seen the bike. "It's a handsome machine, is it not? It was quite a passion of mine for some years, and I couldn't really bring myself to part with it."

"Does Penrose ever ride it?" I asked. "It seems so sad that it should be sitting there unridden."

"Like a high-spirited horse, you mean?" Alec said. "Alas, no. Penrose is not at his best with machinery. He is not particularly stable on four wheels, God knows what he would be like on two!" He gave me a bland smile. "However, he has other qualities."

"Well, he's certainly a brilliant cook," I said, "and you must be so relieved to have someone you can really rely on."

"He's been with me for many years now, first as a dresser, then as cook, chauffeur, valet . . . nurse. He keeps me up to the mark sartorially as well as in every other way."

Certainly Alec was looking very elegant in a lightweight summer suit in a Prince of Wales check, a cream silk shirt, and a Garrick Club tie. The well-polished brogues were hidden as always under the light rug that covered his knees.

I gave a sudden exclamation as the thing that had been eluding me ever since my last visit suddenly sprang clearly to my mind. Alec looked at me in some surprise.

"I'm so sorry," I said, hastily searching around for an excuse for the sound. "I—I caught my finger on the pin of my brooch."

I could see that he didn't believe me, but I was so overwhelmed by the possibility that was now staring me in the face that it hardly seemed important.

With the feeling that I was burning my boats, I said, "It will be a great relief to Bryan and Paul, now that Graham's dead."

He turned and looked at me sharply and I continued. "And you, too, I suppose."

"What exactly do you mean?"

"Josh Brendon wrote me a letter just before he died. Bryan had told him about you all being blackmailed by Graham, and why."

His face was stony. "Indeed?"

"He thought that perhaps I should tell the police."

"And did you?"

"Yes, at least I told Roger Eliot (he's in charge of the case, but he's a friend of mine and very discreet). I told him that Graham was blackmailing you all, though I didn't say why."

"I see."

"It explained why you all put up with Graham, even when he nearly ruined Paul and Bryan."

"Yes."

"And why you let him handle some of your legal affairs, including your divorce, which I assume he somehow bungled."

The expression of passionate fury on his face made me pause for a moment, but I managed to keep my nerve and continued. "So you all had a reason to wish him dead."

"That is true."

"Given his habit of boring on about his activities, you would all have known about the details of his movements, and know when it would be an easy time to kill him."

"I suppose so."

"Bryan and Paul both have alibis for the time that Graham was killed."

"And I?" Alec smiled sardonically and indicated the wheelchair. "Did I somehow contrive to commit a murder in this?"

I ignored his remark and went on. "At first I thought it was Penrose. He's devoted enough, goodness knows, and I don't think he would be too bothered about killing someone who he felt had ruined your life. It was highly unlikely that he would ever be suspected—people don't expect that kind of loyalty from a servant these days! He could have gone down to Taviscombe on the motorbike very early in the morning and probably have been back here to have seen the postman, paid the milkman, or whatever—quite easy to establish an alibi. That bike is very fast. It has also been ridden quite recently."

He raised his eyebrows. "Really?"

"Although the bike is in excellent condition, there is dried mud under the flaps. It happens to be red mud. There is also a coating of lime tree sap on the tank."

"Really?" he repeated.

I took a deep breath and continued.

"It had been raining for several days just before Graham was killed, and there was a lot of mud on the roads round Taviscombe. Red mud. Also, there are lime trees along the part of the Promenade near the spot where Graham was killed, where a bike might have been left."

I paused, but he made no comment.

"Now, there may be some other explanation for these things, but this seems to be the most likely one, don't you think? That whoever rode that bike killed Graham Percy."

Once again the bland smile, the raised eyebrows. I felt him watching as I clasped my hands together to give me confidence to continue. I suppose an actor would notice gestures like that.

"When David and I were here last," I said, and I could hear my own voice high and strained, "we sat for a while in the kitchen chatting to Penrose. While we were chatting, he was cleaning your shoes. He told us that you had a new pair made every year, beautiful shoes, beautifully made, and he showed us the most recent pair. Less than a year old."

He was very tense now.

"The soles were worn and scratched," I said. "They had obviously been worn by someone who was perfectly capable of walking. Now I don't think Penrose had been wearing your shoes on the sly; therefore there can only be one explanation."

I stopped speaking and looked at him. For a moment his eye held mine, then he looked away and gave a little laugh.

"Oh, well," he said. "It had to end sometime, I suppose." With a careless gesture he flung aside the rug and stood up. "You are, of course, absolutely right. I am perfectly capable of walking, capable of riding a motorbike, and capable of killing Graham Percy."

· 18 ·

He was a tall man. I had forgotten how tall he had always appeared on the stage. He seemed to tower over me. It was extraordinary how totally he changed from a sick, elderly man into a middle-aged one, full of a kind of suppressed energy.

"Let's have the lights on." He moved over to the switch and the room was flooded with light. "There, that's better. That depressing half-light, although helpful in the creation of an illusion, is very *wearing*, don't you find?"

I suppose I was still staring at him, bewildered by the sudden transformation, because he laughed and said, "All done with mirrors—no, actually, I'm quite used to playing old men, as you yourself remembered, so I didn't need crepe hair or added wrinkles—just a touch of liner on the back of the hands to emphasize the veins—terribly important, the hands, people don't always realize . . ." He broke off and smiled. "I'm sorry, I won't bore you with technicalities. I suppose I was vain enough to want you to realize what a good performance I gave, without any technical tricks."

"Oh, you were good," I said, "but then you'd played the part before, hadn't you, in *Volpone*? Was that what gave you the idea?"

He stood with his back to the fireplace and regarded me with a mixture of surprise and approval, rather like a schoolmaster whose pupil has unexpectedly answered correctly a difficult question.

"Iago and Volpone," he said, "my two favorite parts, both men who are not what they seem. And yes, you're right, Volpone was my inspiration. The devious Fox, who got what he wanted by pretending to be dying. What did I want? I wanted to kill Graham Percy." He moved over to sit in the chair opposite to mine. "I suppose I must tell you why."

He took a gold cigarette case out of his pocket. "Do you mind if I smoke? I'm too much a child of the forties to give it up entirely."

"No, of course, do smoke."

"Now then, where should I begin? At the beginning, I suppose. I loved Julia very much—no, that's wrong—I loved her *too* much, she was the most important thing in my life, I was obsessed by her. She loved me too, I know that, and deep down she never stopped loving me. Once she went off with someone else, but she came back, as I knew she would. And yet as we grew older I became more impatient, less forgiving about her flirtations. We quarreled, God, how we quarreled! She would fling off in a fury, I would sulk, it was a very turbulent time."

He turned to stub out his half-smoked cigarette. "Then she told me she was in love with Vivian Simon—years younger than she was, but utterly bewitched by her, anyone could see that. I think she was flattered." He gave me a sad little smile. "It would probably have come to nothing, but I put on a tremendous, melodramatic act, told her that if she felt like that she should *go* to him!" He flung out his arm in a mock dramatic gesture.

"So she did. I made no sort of move to get her back. I thought she'd tire of him quite quickly—he was a charming enough boy, but dreadfully boring!—and I suppose that mortified her. She sent me a message through Graham that she wanted a divorce. The very fact that she did it through Graham . . . She didn't know about the blackmail, of course, but she knew I despised him. It was another ploy to irritate me. I knew she was playing some sort of game—she loved playing games with people's emotions—so I didn't take it seriously Right up to the end I played along with it, thinking every day that she'd call it off. But she didn't, and the divorce went through. I couldn't believe it. For months I lived in a sort of daze. Then, quite suddenly, she was dead. That young fool was driving. It wasn't his fault, it was an accident, but she was dead."

I felt a lump in my throat and tears pricking my eyes. He was silent for a moment, his face still and grave. Then he continued, his beautiful voice deliberately flat and emotionless.

"After her death, they sent her things back to me, clothes, books, papers. Among them was her diary. For a while I couldn't bring myself to look at it, but one day I did. She always kept a very full diary, several pages every day, and I discovered from the various entries that she had, indeed, been playing games, that she had been trying to push me to the very edge. But just before the divorce was made final, she had sent a letter to Graham Percy to be forwarded to me. In it, she said that perhaps we should try again and that if I agreed I should meet her on a certain evening at Bertini's—that was our favorite restaurant—to talk about it. She said that if I didn't show up she'd know I didn't want us to get together. I never received that letter."

"But what . . ."

"I never knew what he did with it. Lost it, suppressed it so that the divorce would go through—I don't know. But one thing I do know, if there had been no divorce, Julia would be alive today. *He* killed her, he was responsible for her death."

There seemed nothing that I could say that wouldn't sound trivial, so I was silent.

"I was so *angry*! Not just about Julia's death and his part in it, but for all the years of blackmail—Paul and Bryan as well—all the hateful hypocrisy and deceit. I was angry with myself, too, for not being honest and speaking out, held back by what it might do to us all, and I knew that Bryan and Paul were suffering as well. It all seemed such a God-awful mess, and I felt someone should do something about it. Then I became quite calm and I knew, with absolute certainty, that I would kill Graham Percy because he was a vile creature who shouldn't be allowed to ruin other people's lives as he had ruined mine."

He tapped a cigarette on the gold case, first one end and then the other. "I planned it all with great care. It would be my most brilliant performance, even if it was my last."

I finally found my voice. "How long ago was this?"

"Just over two years." He leaned back in his chair and smiled, a satisfied smile. "It was really very interesting. I built it up very, very slowly. First a slight awkwardness of movement, gradually getting worse, a stiffness, an involuntary grimace at pain stoically borne, you know the kind of thing. Then I began to turn down stage parts, only did cameos in films or television, then let it be known through my agent that I was no longer able to accept any further work. Very convincing, that!" He laughed. "Who'd ever believe that an actor would turn down a job!"

I gave an involuntary smile.

"I enjoyed the challenge," Alec said. "It was fun taking risks. Like Julia, I rather like playing games. Bryan and Paul were easy to fool, but I wondered if David might have rumbled me, after all, he knows all the tricks, but he didn't. Only you . . ."

"You were very good," I said.

He gave me a mock bow in acknowledgment. "I can't think why more actors don't turn to crime," he said lightly. "Not murder, necessarily, but the various kinds of fraud and speculation might offer a rich field."

"We must be grateful," I said, "that they are, by and large, honorable."

"Or unimaginative, or just so obsessed with acting and the theater that they really think or talk of little else. Have you ever heard a group of actors together? Endless stories and anecdotes—the world outside simply doesn't exist."

"So you built up the perfect alibi?"

"Oh, yes, I never lost sight of my ultimate aim."

"Why did you murder Graham in Taviscombe?" I asked.

"I wanted it to be somewhere away from his own home, and I couldn't do it while he was staying with Bryan or Paul, just in case anyone realized that *they* had a motive for wanting him dead. I knew that you or your son could never be suspected. So, I got out the old Norton and drove down in the early hours of the morning. So clever of you to have spotted those things about the bike. I was too overconfident, wasn't I? 'To make a snare for mine own neck!'" he quoted, "'and run my head into it wilfully! With laughter!' Wonderful play, *Volpone*!"

It suddenly seemed to me that he had crossed the line between reality and fantasy, had become a character in a play of his own devising. Questions of justice or morality no longer had any meaning for him.

"Still"—he flung out his arms in a sudden expansive gesture—"it was glorious, riding through the dark and then watching the dawn come up and the early morning light on the sea. I felt so unbelievably *alive*. Then I saw Graham getting out of his car and walking along the Promenade. I'd been waiting in the shelter on the seafront, and as he approached I confronted him. He thought at first I was a mugger—black leathers, helmet—the perfect disguise—but when I raised the visor of my helmet and he saw who it was! God, that was a wonderful moment! A real *coup de théâtre*, you might say! I think he knew then that I was going to kill him, but he was too frightened to call for help, absolutely rigid, like a rabbit with a stoat. Anyway, there was no one about. I didn't say anything. I just stabbed him, took his wallet, and left him on the seat there, quite dead."

He got up and walked back over to the fireplace, leaning his arm along the marble mantelpiece and looking down at me to see how I was taking this confession.

"You threw his wallet into the sea?" I asked.

"Yes, I wanted to make it look like a robbery. I realize now that was a mistake. Obviously I should have taken it right away and destroyed it. One forgets," he said bitterly, "just how treacherous the sea can be."

"They never found the weapon," I said. "They searched the beach, but there was nothing."

"It wasn't on the beach, or indeed in Taviscombe," Alec said, "but back in its rightful place."

He went toward one of the glass cases on the wall and removed an object from it. "Macready's dagger. I have no doubt that, although I wiped it most carefully, a conscientious forensic expert could find traces of Graham Percy's blood on the blade."

I turned and looked at the weapon, but with its ornately chased handle set with mock jewels it looked just like a stage prop, a theatrical memento, part of the world of make-believe, surely not capable of taking a real life.

"Biking leathers are not only a splendid disguise," Alec said in the calm voice of one explaining practicalities," but they are also excellent for not showing the blood." He held out his hands, the dagger still in one of them. " 'A little water clears us of this deed'—I did indeed rinse my hands in the sea—'the multitudinous seas incarnadined, making the green one red.' You see," he said, "how brave I am to be quoting the Scottish play, said, as you know, to be *dreadfully* unlucky. But then, we're not concerned with luck anymore, are we?"

He moved toward me, the dagger still in his hand, and I was suddenly terrified, a rabbit with a stoat, unable to move or say anything. His face was quite near to mine now, the sardonic expression, the arched eyebrows those of Volpone the Fox, the dark eyes unfathomable. Then he turned away and replaced the dagger in its case.

"I'm sorry, my dear," he said gently. "I didn't mean to frighten you—no, that's not quite true. I did. I couldn't resist it, just for a moment. Play-acting again. I apologize."

I realized that I had been holding my breath, and I let it out with a shuddering gasp. I still couldn't take my eyes off him.

He lit another cigarette. "I never intended that anyone else should take the blame for what I'd done. As I say, it had become a game I had to keep up. I always knew that, whether or not anyone found out what I had done, the moment would come when the game would be finished. My life would be finished."

"What do you mean?"

He inhaled deeply and blew out a cloud of smoke. "I have nothing left to live for. Nothing, at least, that I want to live for. An accidental overdose of sleeping tablets, 'After a long illness, bravely borne,' isn't that what they say? You see, my dear, I don't want to go through the rigmarole of a trial, to leave, as it were, a wounded name behind me. Above all, I don't want Penrose involved, as he would be if it all came out."

"Of course, he knew . . ."

"I should, of course, deny that he had any idea that I intended to murder Graham Percy, and that he accepted my fake illness as an eccentricity, a way of escaping from theatrical commitments that had become too great. That, at any rate, is what I've put in the letter."

"The letter?"

"I have written a letter, which I will give to Penrose, explaining everything, only to be used if there is any possibility of anyone else being blamed for the murder. Poor Penrose." He smiled. "I'm leaving him the house, of course, but I expect he will sell it and go and live with his sister in Acton. She used to be a dancer and they fight like cat and dog, but they're fond of each other and it will keep him going. I owe him a lot. He played his part well—he was an actor, you know, before he became my dresser, small parts in weekly rep. . . ." His voice died away and he seemed lost in thought.

Then he turned sharply to me and said briskly, "So you see, it all depends on you."

For a moment I didn't understand what he was saying.

"On me?"

"I'm asking you not to tell the police how you cleverly put two and two together and found the magic number. Will you do that for me? And for Penrose? It's a big thing to ask, I know, but I'm asking it."

"How can I decide—just like that? I need to think . . ."

"Please don't think, just feel."

My instinct was to agree. Who would be harmed if the exact process of the law was evaded in this way? So much misery would be avoided, not just for Penrose, but for all those who, like myself, had admired Alec Patmore and taken such pleasure in his performances. All that would be spoiled, in a way, and all people would remember would be the blaring tabloid headlines. Besides, Paul's and Bryan's situations would be endangered, too. And all for what? This way justice would still be done.

"Very well," I said slowly. "Unless someone else is accused, I will say nothing. I promise."

He let out a great sigh. "Thank you."

He went over to the desk by the window, opened a drawer, and took out a photograph on stiff card.

"I would like you to have this as a small memento," he said. "It is a *carte de visite*."

He handed it to me. It was a picture of Ellen Terry as Portia in the trial scene of *The Merchant of Venice*. The beautiful eyes were glowing with compassion as she faced the court, one hand clutching the bands of her doctor's gown, the other resting lightly on the great book of the Law. Even through the faded sepia the emotion was eloquent. " 'The quality of mercy is not strain'd,' " Alec quoted softly. " 'It droppeth as the gentle rain from heaven upon the place beneath. . . .' "

The moment's silence was broken by Penrose coming into the room. "I'll just clear away the coffee things, and would you like a cup of—" He broke off suddenly as he saw Alec standing by the mantelpiece. "Oh, my God, what's happened?"

Alec went over to him and laid a hand gently on his shoulder.

"It's all right," he said. "It's over, all over."

He turned to me and smiled, the old sardonic smile. "I do hope you'll come to my memorial service. St. Paul's Covent Garden, I imagine. I don't *think* I'd fill St. Martin in the Fields, and it would hardly be an occasion for papering the house."

I felt I had to get home as quickly as possible so I turned onto the motorway. But after driving for a while, I developed a bad headache—not surprising, I suppose—so I drew into a motorway service station. I drank a little tea, crumbled a slice of fruit cake, and tried to eat a little to help down the aspirin I had taken. I found I resented the noise and bustle of the life going on all around me, people eating tea cakes and scones or more substantial kinds of high tea—hamburgers, sausages, baked beans and chips, or even curry—just as if nothing remarkable had happened today. I felt isolated, an alien, some other kind of being.

I took the *carte de visite* from my bag and studied it for a while. Yes, justice *should* be tempered with mercy. I didn't regret the promise I had given. It belonged to a different world, somehow, a world where ordinary rules did not apply. It was a world I had visited many times over the years, one that had given me a great deal of pleasure; the memory of that pleasure was part of my youth, part of my happy married life, and I didn't want it broken or tarnished. Graham or Alec, who was the most worthwhile? Who had given more to life? There was no doubt in my mind.

Tomorrow I would be back in Taviscombe in the real world, helping Rosemary address envelopes for the Church appeal, and in the evening, sitting quietly with my supper on a tray, watching a soap opera. Perhaps it would be more comfortable to live in a soap opera world, where no story line lasts more than a few episodes and where those watching the misery and tragedy therein can banish it by simply turning off a switch.

The girl clearing the tables dumped her tray in front of me. She added my empty cup to the tottering pile already there and stood regarding my half-eaten cake.

"Finished?" she demanded peremptorily.

"Yes, thank you," I said, "quite finished."

Don't miss the next Mrs. Malory mystery,
Mrs. Malory: Death Among Friends,
coming from Signet in 1999.

"Oh Lord!" Rosemary groaned, indicating a sheet of paper cellotaped to the tiles above the sink. "She's at it again!"

I leaned forward to read the notice.

Will the person who removed the rubber gloves from this draining board please return them at once. They are my personal property and are expensive to replace.

Signed Freda Spencer
Chairman, Management Committee

The job of Chairman of the Management Committee of Brunswick Lodge is usually considered to be the sort of thankless task that no one in their right mind would want to be lumbered with. Rosemary and I both agree that the fact that Freda Spencer actively sought the position, indeed seems to revel in it, says a great deal about her character.

Brunswick Lodge, a handsome Georgian building, although owned by the local council is leased at a peppercorn rent to the Friends, who run it as a sort of up-market community center, with concerts, play-readings and such mild cultural activities as Taviscombe is prepared to accept. It is also a popular venue for jumble and bring-and-buy sales and there is a sort of permanent exhibition of pictures and artifacts relating to Old Taviscombe in what is grandly, if erroneously, known as the Museum Room. There is a non-resident caretaker, Mr. Soames, an unhelpful man who is supposed to keep the place clean, but doesn't, and the house is generally maintained by volunteers.

As anyone who has ever tried to run *anything* with the help of volunteers will know, it is not easy. A very high standard of tact and diplomacy, if not downright sycophancy, is essential if personalities are not to clash and umbrage is not to be taken. Unfortunately, Freda Spencer, though possessed of many other qualities necessary for a successful leader (perseverance, determination and downright bossiness) is palpably lacking in the gentler arts and, since her elevation to the Chair, has managed to alienate a fair number of useful helpers.

"Oh dear," Rosemary said, "I wish she wouldn't! There'll be nobody left at all if she goes on like this! Poor Lilian Baker was almost in tears because Freda was so beastly to her when she forgot to turn the lights out in the committee room and they were left on all night—a mistake anyone could make. And Jack says that Maureen Philips is thinking of resigning from the Committee because of the way Freda rides roughshod over everyone's suggestions."

Rosemary's husband Jack is also on the Committee and, being a man who has no inhibitions about expressing himself forcefully, has had some notable battles with Freda.

"I know," I agreed. "It is difficult. But she *does* get things done, you must admit—remember how run-down everything was before she took over?"

"Yes, I know all that, but Freda really is the limit!"

"Oh, I agree, she's the end! But, honestly, who on earth would take on the job if she didn't do it?"

There being no reply to this, Rosemary remained silent.

"And really," I continued, "her energy's quite re-markable, considering she must be in her late seventies by now. I just wish I had half her vitality!"

"Just think," Rosemary said, "what she must have been like in the war."

Freda Spencer, as she never tires of telling anyone who will listen, had been an officer in the WRNS. Her brisk manner certainly brings with it more than a hint of the quarterdeck and her conversation is still sprinkled with service slang. It is obvious that she has every intention of running Brunswick Lodge as a tight ship.

"Well, you know people are so vague and woolly-minded," I said, "they really do sometimes need a bomb behind them to get things done."

"I can't think why you're defending her," Rosemary protested, "when you know you can't stand the woman."

The sound of the kitchen door opening made us both swing round guiltily. But it was only Sybil Jacobs, who loathes Freda even more than we do.

"Hello, what's this then?" she said, coming over to the sink. "Yet another of Freda's notices? Oh, I think that was me. I used them when I washed up after the coffee morning on Wednesday. I put them away in this drawer here." She opened the drawer by the sink and took out a pair of yellow rubber gloves and laid them with some solemnity on the draining board. "There. Now perhaps her ladyship will be satisfied. Honestly! what a fuss about nothing. Typical of Freda!"

Rosemary sighed. "Talking about a fuss about nothing, Jack says she was banging on about having tighter security everywhere—locks on windows, special fastenings on doors, that sort of thing. It'll cost a fortune! Derek Forster told her the money simply wasn't available, but she wouldn't listen, you know how she is. She just tanked over him and now *he's* offended and we'll never get another treasurer half as good!"

"It's absolutely ridiculous!" Sybil said roundly. "Apart from a bit of petty cash there's nothing worth stealing here, anyway. Unless"—her voice took on a satirical tone—"Freda thinks that the objects in the Museum Room might attract the attention of a gang of international art thieves!"

"I suppose," Rosemary said, "she was thinking of

vandals breaking in and doing a lot of damage. There was that business down by the seafront. . . ."

"A few yobbos who've had too much to drink breaking up a bus shelter isn't the same thing at all," Sybil protested. "Anyway, there are perfectly good folding wooden shutters on the downstairs windows."

"I know. But you know what Freda's like once she's got her teeth into something—she's not going to let up. She'll make everyone's life a misery until she gets her own way."

"Oh well," I said resignedly, "we'll just have to see. Now then, could you both very kindly give me a hand to lug this box of books upstairs?"

Rosemary and I were in Brunswick Lodge making preparations for the Christmas Fayre held every first Saturday in December since time immemorial. Rosemary had the produce stall and I (because of my vague connection with literature) was in charge of the book stall.

"Oh, just a minute," Sybil said to Rosemary. "I must just hand over this jam and lemon curd." She started to unload a quantity of jars from her shopping basket onto the worktop.

"Oh, lovely!" I said. "I adore lemon curd and it's so tedious to make—all that stirring in double saucepans! It's very popular, it goes in a flash. I must make sure I get in early."

"Take a jar now," Sybil said.

"No, I mustn't," I protested. "I'm always complaining about the way helpers grab the best things for themselves before the public get a look in."

"Oh, don't be silly! Here—if it makes your conscience feel any better, take this jar as a personal present from me to you and then you can make a suitable contribution to funds in general. How's that?"

"A very persuasive piece of sophistry." I laughed, taking the jar and putting it in my bag. "Thank you very much."

Rosemary, who had been turning over some of the books in the box, held up a couple of depressing looking volumes. "*Electrical Wiring for Beginners* and a life of Annie Besant! Who on earth will buy those?"

"You never know," I said. "Some young couple doing up their first home who just happen to be theosophists . . ."

"Why do we never get some rare first edition?" Rosemary asked. "Or even," she continued more practically, "some decent detective paperbacks?"

"There's a lovely big pile of Mills and Boon," I said, rummaging about in the box. "They always go well. And several cookery books."

"Oh, let me look," Sybil said. "No, that's no good—Indian and Mexican. Pauline would never eat anything like that. Her idea of adventurous eating is a Spanish omelette!"

Pauline is Sybil's twin sister. Since they were both widowed they now share a house, and, although they are really devoted to each other, they seem obliged to take up diametrically opposite views on absolutely everything. Rosemary says it's the only way they can assert their individuality, which is probably true, but it's very wearing for all their friends.

"I'll never forget how absolutely maddening she was in Rome that time," Sybil went on. "I could scarcely get her out of that English tea-room by the Spanish Steps. And asking for thinly sliced bread and butter, if you please, when we were in Doney's in Florence!"

Although they are now both well into their seventies, Sybil and Pauline are still keen travellers, bickering their way around the globe with great enthusiasm. Not only to the usual tourist places, but also to less frequented bits of the Middle and even the Far East where thin bread and butter is, I imagine, quite unobtainable.

"Where are you going next year?" I asked.

"We thought Calabria. Start at the bottom and work upwards to Naples. I'd like to see Naples again. I was there in the war—it's probably quite spoilt now. Funnily enough, Freda was in Naples too, a lot of Wrens were, but not at the same time as me, thank God! At least, I never ran across her."

"I didn't know you were in the Wrens, Sybil," I said.

"No, Pauline and I were nurses, Queen Alexandra's, quite the best thing to be in. You got sent absolutely everywhere."

"Were you together all the time, you and Pauline?" Rosemary asked.

"At first we were. We joined the FANYs at the beginning of the war. God! That was a wonderfully crazy set-up in those days. I once found myself driving an Admiral of the Fleet in full dress uniform across Salisbury Plain in a racing car in a snow storm—but that's a long story. Then after a bit we transferred to the QA's and Pauline went to India and I went to South Africa—Simonstown—and then Gibraltar, and ended up in Naples. That's where I met Maurice."

"Fantastic," Rosemary said, "England must have seemed pretty tame after that."

"Well, I wasn't here all that long. Maurice was in the Foreign Office, so we moved about quite a bit. But when he died and Pauline was on her own too, we somehow both drifted back to Taviscombe. You know how it is."

"It's funny, really," I said, "how many people *have* come back. There's you and Pauline. And Freda, too, for that matter. And Leslie and Jean Evans and Matthew and Elizabeth Fenchurch and Richard Lewis—oh, heaps of people!"

"All coming back to their roots," Rosemary said. "I suppose it's something you do when you're getting older. It's nice for us old stick-in-the-muds who never left the place. Makes us feel we made the right choice after all!"

"Well, quite a lot of people who went away will

be coming back in January," I remarked. "The school reunion, remember?"

"Goodness, yes," Rosemary said. "I must send in our form for the dinner. Let's all try and sit together. Last time Jack and I were stuck at a table with Alan Watson and that awful wife of his. *He* gave us a ball-by-ball description of every game of golf he's ever played and she went on and on about this apartment they have in Spain. Jack was barely civil by the end of the evening."

"Oh yes, please, I'd like that," I said gratefully. As a female on my own I have been landed only too often with uncongenial dinner companions.

"You can count us in too," Sybil said. "But won't Jack mind being the only man surrounded by four females?"

"He'd enjoy it," Rosemary laughed. "But I suppose I could ask Richard Lewis to even things up a bit. He's not exactly a sparkling conversationalist but he's a nice old thing."

"Oh, I expect *he'll* want to be sitting with Freda," Sybil said. "He's always hanging round her."

"That's true, he really is devoted."

"Has been for years," Sybil agreed. "I think Freda found him quite useful when she first came back to Taviscombe, after Bill retired. And of course she used him as a sort of unpaid nursemaid for Bill when he had that second stroke, and then when *he* died Richard was handy to do things around the house and take her out to dinner. Poor sap!" She sniffed derisively. "But his nose must be right out of joint now."

"You mean Laurence?" Rosemary asked.

Instinctively we all drew closer together and lowered our voices. Laurence Marvell was Freda's new constant companion. As far as we could judge, he was in his mid-forties, very good-looking with thick dark hair and a tall, elegant figure, impeccably dressed in a rather theatrical way (double-breasted waistcoat, velvet collar on his coat) and with the most charming manners. All this would have been unusual enough in this day and age, but what marked him out in Taviscombe (conservative in every sense of the word) was that he made no secret of the fact that he was gay. Although he frequently referred to his friend Jimmy, it looked as if that relationship was now in the past and he seemed to have no present attachment. Unless you counted his continual dancing attendance on Freda.

"Of course, she *pays* for everything," Rosemary said. "When they go anywhere—out to dinner or the theater in London or that trip to Paris for lunch on the Shuttle. I suppose that's the attraction."

"She certainly seems besotted," I said. "It was Larry this and Larry that the last time I saw her."

"It's disgusting!" Sybil said gruffly. "Surely she must see that she's making a fool of herself and people are laughing at her behind her back."

"It would never occur to Freda that anyone would *dare* to laugh at her, even behind her back," I said.

"Well, they do," Sybil persisted. "Even Olive was talking about it the other day, and you know how loyal she usually is?"

Olive is Freda's cousin. They were more or less brought up together, although Olive remained in Taviscombe, looking after her father when her mother died quite young. Of course they kept in touch and then when Freda came back here she co-opted Olive as a sort of lady-in-waiting. Olive, being quite different from her cousin, meekly acquiesced and was usually to be found one step behind Freda on most occasions. The fact that Olive had actually voiced concern showed how far things must have gone.

"He really is wonderfully civil," Rosemary said dreamily. "Exquisitely polite, lovely old-fashioned manners one had thought were gone forever."

"Oh, yes," I agreed. "I can quite see how anyone could be bewitched—it's just the fact that it's Freda that makes it so remarkable."

"Where did he spring from, anyway?" Sybil demanded.

"I think he was a schoolmaster somewhere in London," I said. "I don't know where. Freda told me he took early retirement on health grounds."

"He looks healthy enough to me," Sybil snorted, "and I wonder who pays for his clothes. You can't tell me a retired schoolmaster could afford that overcoat; its Aquascutum. I saw the label when he took it off at the concert last week."

"Yes," Rosemary agreed," and that was a Ralph

Lauren polo shirt he was wearing the other day. I saw the little logo thing."

"Perhaps Freda bought them for him," I suggested. "She's pretty comfortably off."

"In that case," Sybil demanded, "why doesn't she do more for that wretched daughter of hers?"

Freda's only child, Emily, had made an unwise marriage against her mother's wishes. She was a very pretty girl, with Freda's dark, curly hair, great brown eyes, and slim figure, and it was fairly obvious that Freda (who was a bit of a snob) had hoped for some sort of grand alliance, or at least a marriage into one of the professions. Instead, when Emily was at Cambridge she had fallen in love with another student, Ben Merrick—not the scion of a noble house with endless acres, but the son of a toolmaker in the Midlands, with no money and no prospects. Freda had forbidden the match but, in the first and most devastating rebellious act of her life, Emily had married Ben anyway. He had ideas about self-sufficiency and ecological correctness and they had ended up on a tiny smallholding in Devon, which Emily bought with a legacy from her father. I think they were happy together but, with very little money, it was a distinctly Spartan existence. Freda had very publicly declared her intention of washing her hands of the whole affair and the phrase "made her own bed and now she must lie on it" was bandied about from time to time whenever Freda remembered past injustices she deemed had been done to her.

Olive, who had never married, had always been very fond of Emily and had, she once confided in me, been surreptitiously sending what money she could to support the young couple, who had compounded their imprudence in Freda's eyes by having three children very close together.

"You'd think, wouldn't you," Rosemary said, "that Freda would have some sort of feeling for her grandchildren? I don't think she's ever even *seen* them."

To Rosemary, who dotes on and is deeply involved with her own two grandchildren, this is quite the most incomprehensible part of the whole affair.

"She probably doesn't want dear Laurence to think of her as a grandmother," Sybil said sardonically. "She's always buzzing about like a two-year-old!"

"Well, as we were saying before," I said, "she really is amazing for her age. She's still remarkably handsome."

And she is. Tall and upright, with her dark hair only lightly (and attractively) streaked with gray, and, since she has that pale, very thick skin that never seems to show the wrinkles, she doesn't look anything like her age. She spends a lot on clothes, too, and is a constant (and favored) customer of Taviscombe's only fashionable dress shop, Estelle's, as well as getting a lot of her things in Bath and Exeter or even London. In fact, it is the times when Freda sends in some of her cast-offs for a jumble sale that the helpers really do descend like locusts to have the first pick before the public can get at them.

"Handsome is as handsome does!" Sybil has never hesitated to express her feelings by means of a cliché. "She's far too full of herself and I, for one, look forward to the day when someone takes her down a peg. Pride," she added, with the air of one making an original statement, "goes before a fall."